CAVANAUGH

JOSHUA KORNREICH

Sagging
Meniscus

Printed in Great Britain and the United States of America.
Set in Minion with LaTeX.

ISBN: 978-1-952386-14-5 (paperback)
ISBN: 978-1-952386-15-2 (ebook)
Library of Congress Control Number: 2021944399

Sagging Meniscus Press
Montclair, New Jersey
saggingmeniscus.com

To pitchers and belly-itchers

CONTENTS

CAVANAUGH

CAVANAUGH IS NOT KAVANAUGH

IT HAD BEEN HIBERNATING on and off inside his head for years. It was a thing, a voice—a living, breathing voice—a voice separate and distinct from his own voice. He had at first mistaken it for the voice of someone else in the rows of stadium seats surrounding him, but now, after a long hiatus, it—this thing, this voice—had reemerged from its cerebral dugout, refreshed and replenished, alien yet familiar.

"Play ball," said the voice.

The man whose head this voice was inside of—they called him Cavanaugh, and he was, more or less, much like everyone else: a pencil-pusher, a number-cruncher, a middling middle-aged middle-man who never had an agenda in life other than to provide for his wife and child. He was fair-skinned and freckled, pockmarked and birthmarked, made of the same make as his forebears before him. The hair on his head was no longer the flowing dark mane that was once the envy of friend and foe alike, but rather a clumpy, thinning tumbleweed of silver and beige. While his chest was still broad, it had gone soft in recent years, and though his midsection had evolved into what his wife affectionately referred to as his "man-pouch," Cavanaugh was a man who, despite the odds, remained comfortable under his own layers of pasty flab. His eyes were a chestnut brown, and though his long-range vision was on a slow and steady decline, Cavanaugh was still able to see Kavanaugh from afar with sufficient clarity, as the latter took a slow yet confident trot toward the diamond and waved to the cheering crowd.

Let it be clear: Cavanaugh was not Kavanaugh.

And let this also be clear: Kavanaugh was not Cavanaugh.

Yet, regardless of what their respective virtues and shortcomings were, it was Kavanaugh, not Cavanaugh, who had been bestowed the honor of delivering the night's ceremonial first pitch.

The crowd roared for Kavanaugh as he took the field.

The crowd did not roar for Cavanaugh as he took another large bite into his stadium-length hot dog. In fact, the only person in the whole stadium who paid him any mind at that moment was his young, red-haired, freckle-faced daughter—the apple of his eye—who spoke softly and sweetly in his ear as he went about his chewing.

"Can I have one of those?" She pointed to a bobblehead doll being held in the lap of a toddler in the row in front of them. She then pointed to an identical bobblehead doll to the left of the toddler, then to another identical one to the right, and then to yet another appearing larger-than-life on the giant digital billboard behind centerfield.

Little heads bobbled all around Cavanaugh.

Cavanaugh decided to respond to his daughter's request just like any good American dad with a mouthful of hot dog would: "What for?" he said.

It was not that Cavanaugh had not wanted to buy his daughter another doll. After all, there was nothing wrong with her wanting another doll, and despite her being in possession of so many other dolls already, Cavanaugh did not see the harm in letting her add yet another to her vast collection.

Plus, this was a different kind of doll from the ones she already had—this was a bobblehead, or a nodder, as some in the know might say—so, to let her have this particular doll would not be, in his eyes, spoiling her in any substantive manner.

Besides, he figured it was only a matter of minutes before her friend's father, O'Reilly, who was sitting right next to them, would end up buying the bobblehead for *his* own daughter to add to *her* undoubtedly vast doll collection. Thus, his thinking went, if he himself should feel guilty about carrying out such an act, then they would *both* have to feel guilty.

But why would either father feel burdened with any sort of guilt about purchasing yet another doll for his daughter on a night such as this, when the four of them—the two fathers and their respective daughters—were having such a fun and memorable night out on the town? They were sitting only a few rows behind their favorite minor league team's dugout on a pleasantly mild summer night, feasting on crackerjacks, soft pretzels, french fries, ice cream, cotton candy, and anything else their wallets could accommodate.

Cavanaugh knew that O'Reilly already had guzzled down two or three beers too many as it was—all before the opening pitch—but, to Cavanaugh, that was okay: it was the bus that was driving them home that night, not O'Reilly. While he was not surprised that O'Reilly's daughter hardly seemed to pay any mind to her father's excessive drinking—he figured she had probably grown accustomed to it over the years—he did have some concern about his own daughter seeing O'Reilly in the deeply inebriated condition he was in. But neither girl, sitting between the one father that was sober and the one that was not, seemed to take notice, or at least show any hint of unease.

As for Cavanaugh himself, it had been years since he had given up drinking, so when it came to dealing with big drinkers like O'Reilly, his feelings ranged between empathy and contempt.

But, for Cavanaugh, it was not the risk of spoiling his daughter with a bobblehead that was irking him so much now, was it?

No, it was not. It was the *likeness* of the bobblehead—that was what was irking him. For Cavanaugh knew, even then, that the voice of the announcer blaring over the stadium loudspeaker would linger in his head and haunt him for days to come.

Ladies and gentlemen, it is now time for tonight's ceremonial first pitch. Heading now to the mound is one of the great patriots of our time and one of the true protectors of our freedom. He is fresh off the bench of the Supreme Court of the United States. Will you all please rise and give a warm hero's welcome . . . Ladies and gentlemen, here he is, defender of our Constitution . . . Justice . . . Brett . . . Kavanaugh.

Cavanaugh's daughter turned to Cavanaugh. "Cavanaugh? Did he just say Cavanaugh, Daddy? Was he a famous player or something? Do you think we're related?"

O'Reilly chuckled hard at this, the kernels of his crackerjacks spewing out of his mouth as he chuckled.

Cavanaugh looked over the girls' heads, his eyes meeting squarely with O'Reilly's own.

"Hey, O'Reilly—did you know about this?"

"Know about what?"

"That tonight was Brett Kavanaugh Night?"

"I didn't until I saw those bobbleheads on the way to the john—got my little girl one."

Just then, O'Reilly put his hand into a white plastic bag and pulled out a bobblehead whose likeness was that of the justice, only this Brett Kavanaugh was not clad in his usual judicial attire, but instead was wearing the uniform of a minor league ballplayer, with a shiny red cap on his oversized head, and a pocket-sized bat in his tiny grip.

But it was Kavanaugh, alright, smirk and all.

"Is that for me, Daddy?" asked the O'Reilly girl.

"It sure is, angel."

"Aw, thanks! You're the best dad ever!"

As the O'Reilly girl gave O'Reilly a great big hug, the latter gave Cavanaugh a Kavanaugh-esque wink.

"Daddy! Daddy!" said Cavanaugh's daughter. "Can I have one, too? Can I? Can I?"

"What do you need one for?"

"Oh, come on, Cavanaugh," said O'Reilly. "It's your own daughter, for christ sake."

Cavanaugh shot a mild glare at O'Reilly, then said: "So, you think I should actually get her one?"

"Why not?"

Cavanaugh knew that when it came to the subject of Brett Kavanaugh, there were those who believed that he was a sociopathic sexual predator and those who believed he was an unjustly vilified umpire of the law, and that when it came to those two opposing viewpoints, there was a high degree of correlation between the viewpoint held and where the holder of such a viewpoint fell within the spectrum of the political mainstream. Cavanaugh, for one, more or less held the former viewpoint, but he was not one to ruminate about such injustices when it came to justices, for he figured that when it came to justices and those put in charge of nominating and confirming such justices, that they all, more or less, must have, at some point, committed sexual assault themselves over the course of their own private lives, for why would one tolerate such a gross injustice otherwise?

Nevertheless, Cavanaugh tried to respond to O'Reilly's direct question in a way as to avert a political or moral discussion—especially given the elevated level of O'Reilly's inebriety.

"Well, for one, she doesn't need another doll—she already has more dolls than anyone could count."

"Doll?" said O'Reilly. "This ain't no doll. It's a bobblehead. And what's better, it's one of them *electronic* bobbleheads. See, when you push the button on its base there, the head starts snapping super-duper fast. Why, this thing here—heck, it's a steal, Cavanaugh. It'll probably be a collector's item someday."

Cavanaugh's daughter's face lit up. "You hear that, Daddy? It's going to be a collector's item someday. Please, pretty please, can I have one? Pretty, pretty please? Pretty, pretty, pretty please?"

Cavanaugh sighed as the real Brett Kavanaugh removed his baseball cap and waved it at the crowd after hurling what appeared to be a surprisingly perfect slider. As the crowd cheered, the toddler with the bobblehead sitting in the row in front of Cavanaugh removed her own cap from her head, and waved it back at the justice.

A man and a woman shouted behind Cavanaugh in unison: "We love you, Brett!"

Surrounded by cheers and applause, Cavanaugh thought he might just go ahead and hurl one out himself—not a baseball though, but rather his own guts.

"Hey, Cavanaugh," whispered O'Reilly, as the two men's daughters were transfixed with what was transpiring on the mound. "Don't get your knickers in a knot. She'll just think it's some ballplayer or something. Trust me. She'll never know."

O'Reilly winked again.

Somehow, O'Reilly's cockeyed logic made sense to Cavanaugh, so he decided to go along with it, and on the way back from the men's restroom in the middle of the third inning, Cavanaugh pulled out his wallet and purchased a pint-sized Brett Kavanaugh for his beloved freckle-faced angel.

And with that, all was right with the world.

In the bottom of the fifth, Cavanaugh saw the same toddler in the row in front of him give her Brett Kavanaugh bobblehead a kiss on the nose.

How cute, thought Cavanaugh. Probably just for good luck.

No one said anything about Brett Kavanaugh or Brett Kavanaugh's likeness for the rest of the night—neither for the remainder of the game, nor during the long bus ride home in which O'Reilly snored all the way through until his daughter punched him hard enough in the shoulder to jostle him awake when they had arrived at their stop.

After lumbering off the bus, O'Reilly and the O'Reilly girl walked a few paces ahead of Cavanaugh and his daughter, their two-story house only a few houses away from the stop. When they reached the O'Reilly house, O'Reilly fumbled about the pockets of his pants for several seconds before finding his keys and giving Cavanaugh a no-look thumbs-up.

Cavanaugh watched O'Reilly limp up the driveway toward the front door of his house, and wondered: Was the limp something O'Reilly had always had? Was it from a leg injury from long ago, from way back in his childhood perhaps? Or maybe he had had it since birth—a genetic defect of sorts. Or perhaps it was simply a byproduct of the kind of life in which O'Reilly had indulged, the cumulative effect of a lifetime's worth of guzzling down copious amounts of alcohol now manifesting itself as some sort of neuromuscular ailment.

The two girls exchanged goodbyes, then onward the two Cavanaughs went, father and child, the moon following them stealthily through the trees as they made their way home.

Somewhere down the road, a dog barked.

CAVANAUGH COUNTS CAVANAUGHS

CAVANAUGH HEARD THE CREAKING of footsteps coming from the upstairs hallway even before his wife opened the door.

"She's so sweet," whispered Mrs. Cavanaugh to her husband as she entered their master bedroom and quietly closed the door behind her. "She wanted to sleep with that bobblehead doll you got her. I told her that the make of the doll was too hard for her to sleep with, that she might hurt herself sleeping with it, but then I told her we could keep it on her nightstand, and it'll watch over her as she sleeps. She seemed to take to that idea, so that's where the doll is right now—right on that nightstand, watching over her." Mrs. Cavanaugh pulled down the comforter and cozied up to her husband in bed. "By the way, who's that doll supposed to be anyway? There's something vaguely familiar about it."

Cavanaugh thought for a moment about how to reply, then said: "I'm not sure if it's supposed to be anyone. Just a player on the team, I think. No one specific."

"Well, it's a cute doll."

"Cute doll? Is that what you just said? Cute doll?"

"Yeah. Why?"

"Well, what's so cute about it?"

"I don't know. Its head—the way it moves, I guess."

"Oh. Okay."

"Why? Are you jealous?" Mrs. Cavanaugh reached out under the covers and gave Cavanaugh the tickles, but Cavanaugh did not like getting the tickles from Mrs. Cavanaugh—at least not right at that moment—so Cavanaugh turned over to the other said of the bed and shut his eyes.

"Jeez," said Mrs. Cavanaugh. "What's gotten into you? Was it a bad game or something? Was O'Reilly acting up again?"

Cavanaugh wasn't quite sure about the overall quality of the game he had just witnessed. Seeing Brett Kavanaugh on the mound, throwing that slider—well, that was enough to throw him off his own game, disrupting his concentration for the rest of the night.

So, he went with one of her other questions: "Yeah. It was O'Reilly. It was him."

"Oh, that's too bad. His daughter though—she's so nice. What's her name again?"

"The O'Reilly girl."

"Yeah, I know she's O'Reilly's girl. But what's her name?"

"The O'Reilly girl. That's her name. That's the name I see whenever I see her name in my head: the O'Reilly girl."

"Funny, Cavanaugh. Real funny."

As he lay on his side in the dark beside her, Cavanaugh thought about all the times Mrs. Cavanaugh addressed him as Cavanaugh instead of by his first name whenever she was upset with him or over something he had said. After a few minutes of counting from their first date onward, he drifted into unconsciousness.

CAVANAUGH HEARS ANOTHER VOICE

A VOICE both sinister and familiar echoed in Cavanaugh's ears, stirring him in his sleep.

"What goes around, comes around," said the voice.

Cavanaugh shot up from his bed. It only took him half a moment to realize that it had just been the tail-end of a late-night dream gone awry, and that the voice he had heard had come not from one of the dark corners of the bedroom, but from inside his own head. And it took him just a half-moment more to realize that the voice sounded a lot like the voice of Brett Kavanaugh—or at least that was how it sounded to him anyway.

But the voice was not the voice of Brett Kavanaugh. Nor was it the voice of the Brett Kavanaugh bobblehead doll sitting on the nightstand in the bedroom across the upstairs hallway of his house—the doll that was now, as Mrs. Cavanaugh put it, "watching over" their young child.

But the voice did *sound* like the voice of Brett Kavanaugh.

Cavanaugh stared up at the ceiling, though he could not see it in the dark. *I have a voice living inside my head that sounds like the voice of a Supreme Court justice.*

The thought chilled Cavanaugh, unsettled him. His eyes were weary, but he would not dare to close them again.

He turned over and studied his wife's face, pockmarked like his own, as she snored soundly in her sleep.

Mrs. Cavanaugh.

That was the name for his wife he kept seeing in his head whenever he saw her or thought about her.

Mrs. Cavanaugh.

Her first name, let alone her maiden name, had already faded far into the background of his mind, so far that he could now only see her in his head as Mrs. Cavanaugh.

Cavanaugh kept his eyes on Mrs. Cavanaugh as he quietly rolled out of bed, careful as not to wake her. It was dark in the room, but there was enough moonlight eking out from around the edges of the window shade that he still had his bearings. He made his way to the door, and tiptoed into the hallway, toward the bedroom of his only child.

I need to check on her, he thought. He knew it was ridiculous to think she was not all right—after all, it was just a lifeless bobblehead doll watching over her, was it not?—but since he was already up anyway, why not take a look?

He turned the doorknob of her door carefully, trying his best to mitigate its creak. As the door slowly swung open, he half-expected to see the doll looking right at him with a taunting smirk, its head bobbling maniacally up and down.

But when he looked over at the nightstand, there it was, serene and still in the almost-pitch-black of the room, facing in the direction of his daughter whose head was turned to the far wall as she slept soundly under the covers.

Watching over her, he thought, just as Mrs. Cavanaugh had described.

Cavanaugh tiptoed back out of the room and shut the door behind him as quietly as he came in. He was thirsty and not quite ready to return to his bedroom, so instead he crept down the staircase at the far end of the hallway, and headed toward the kitchen.

"I could use a drink," whispered the voice inside his head.

Hearing the voice say this unnerved Cavanaugh. It was something it had not said to him in years.

The voice spoke again, this time louder: "I could use a drink."

Cavanaugh decided to ignore it. When he reached the kitchen, he could see a light flashing on and off on the counter. It was his smartphone, and he could tell from where he stood that there was a text message on it. He walked over to the phone, picked it up, and read the message.

It was from O'Reilly: *Call me*, it said.

Cavanaugh looked up from his phone and thought about what this message from O'Reilly could mean. Was he still drunk? Had he fallen ill from being drunk? If so, why would he call him at this hour? He had a wife, after all. A wife and a young daughter, just like Cavanaugh.

In the dark of the kitchen, Cavanaugh's thoughts went to dark places. Maybe O'Reilly had done something wrong, or was about to do something wrong to himself. Maybe that is why he wants to talk to me, thought Cavanaugh, instead of talking it out with his wife, who probably was asleep right next to him.

Or, perhaps she was not asleep right next to him. Maybe she had run out on him. Maybe she had run out on him along with their daughter.

Or, maybe, thought Cavanaugh, maybe O'Reilly had killed his wife and daughter, and he wants my help in covering it up.

"I could use a drink," said the voice.

Cavanaugh put the phone back down on the counter and opened the refrigerator door.

Then he closed the refrigerator door.

He looked back at his phone. It was no longer flashing.

He wanted no part of whatever O'Reilly had to say, but he had to know. He had to know what was behind the text.

Like the bobblehead, he thought. I'm just checking it out. Just a simple dotting of the i's and crossing of the t's.

"Lives might be at stake," said the voice.

He picked up the phone and dialed O'Reilly's number. It was answered on the first ring.

"Hey," said O'Reilly.

"Hey, what's going on, man?"

"Figured you'd still be up."

"Oh, yeah? Why's that?"

"Come on, man. You know why."

"Know why what?"

"Let's just talk about it calmly here, okay? Like two civilized grown-ups."

"Huh? Talk about what?"

"Kavanaugh. The doll."

Cavanaugh swallowed hard. He wished he had ignored the message and never called.

"What about the doll?" said Cavanaugh. He couldn't bring himself to say the doll's surname out loud despite it having the exact same pronunciation as his own.

"It bothers you, the doll," said O'Reilly. His voice was whispery, yet penetrating. There was a sense of relish behind it. "Admit it, man. It bothers you that people paid good money for this doll, that they bought it for all their little kiddies to take home with them. It freaks you out that those little kiddies are all now tucked in their little beds, sleeping with a doll that resembles Brett Kavanaugh. Am I right or am I right?"

Cavanaugh thought about what O'Reilly said for a moment, swallowed hard again, then spoke: "Well, my daughter isn't sleeping with *her* doll tonight. It's on her nightstand."

"Watching over her," said the voice.

The voice was so loud now in his head that Cavanaugh wondered if O'Reilly could hear it himself.

"And how would you know that?" said O'Reilly. "How would you know she's not sleeping with it? Did you go into her bedroom and check?"

This line of questioning stunned Cavanaugh, as much for its instinctiveness as for its invasiveness. It was as if the alcohol O'Reilly had imbibed earlier had magically instilled in him a sense of probing insight into how the human mind actually works when confronted with anxiety. But Cavanaugh wasn't going to let O'Reilly have the upper hand.

"Why does it matter to you?" said Cavanaugh.

"You did, didn't you? You went in and checked. You went in and checked because you were scared."

"Scared? Scared of what?"

"Of the doll. Or maybe not really the doll, but of what your daughter having that doll—you know, getting all cozy with it under the covers—would mean."

There was a silence on the phone. O'Reilly was right, but Cavanaugh wasn't going to let him know it.

"Well, what about *your* daughter then?"

"What about her?"

Cavanaugh wasn't exactly comfortable using O'Reilly's daughter as a weapon against O'Reilly in order to turn the tables on him, but he proceeded nonetheless. "Is *she* sleeping with it?"

"With *him*, you mean?"

Cavanaugh could sense O'Reilly's insistence on making this as uncomfortable for him as possible. He had been the target of O'Reilly's passive-aggression on previous occasions, but not in such blatant fashion. Perhaps this was part of the alcohol talking.

I could use a drink.

"Well, yeah," said Cavanaugh. "With him. Is she sleeping with him?"

"Well, fuck me, man," said O'Reilly. "Of course she's sleeping with him!"

Cavanaugh felt a queasy twinge in his gut. He imagined his own daughter sleeping with the doll. Or, worse yet, rubbing herself off against it like kids her age sometimes do with their stuffed animals.

Cavanaugh knew he needed to put an end to the conversation and quickly, before it unraveled even further. He cleared his throat and began to speak: "Okay, well—"

"Hey, do you have a fucking problem with that?"

"Excuse me?"

"Do you have a fucking problem with me letting my daughter sleep with her Brett Kavanaugh doll?"

"A problem?"

"I bet you do, Cavanaugh. I bet you do have a problem with it, but you think you're too good to say something about it, right? You and that fucking high-and-mighty-I-quit-drinking-uppity attitude of yours."

"Attitude? Hey, man, I don't know what you're talking about—"

"You think he raped those women, don't you? You're like everybody else, all those fake media people. You think Kavanaugh raped them all, right?"

"Well, yeah, I think he might have done that—yes."

"Oh, that figures. That figures, Cavanaugh, that you—someone like you—would think that, that you would say that. But so what? But so what if he did?"

"So what if he did? Is that what you're saying? So what if he did?" Cavanaugh could feel the rage brewing within himself. He never liked O'Reilly. It was just that their daughters were friends that he tolerated him. O'Reilly was just someone that he had to put up with.

"Yeah," said O'Reilly. "That is what I'm fucking saying. And so-the-fuck what? So-the-fuck what he if he fucking raped all those fucking women that he raped? So-the-fuck what?"

Cavanaugh could not believe his ears for a moment, but then remembered O'Reilly lumbering his way up his driveway. Perhaps this was just him overcompensating for his pathetic limp.

"Well, doesn't that bother you at all?"

"Bother me?" said O'Reilly. "Does it bother me? Hey, man, haven't you ever done something like that to a girl, or, I mean, a woman before?"

"Done something like what?"

"You know, like, not like *rape* maybe, but maybe gone a little further than you should've?"

Cavanaugh was about to say no, but something held him back. What was it?

There was a quiet pause on the phone, a pause that was longer than Cavanaugh had wished.

I could use a drink.

"Ha! So, you *have* done something like that," said O'Reilly.

"Done what?"

"Gone a little further than you should've—you have, right? Aw, man, you *have*! Probably some long time ago, right?"

"No, man. You're not right. That's not what I—"

"Was it one time? Was it one time you did it? Or was it more than one time? Which was it?"

"Dude, you're fucking crazy."

"Well, son of a bitch, Cavanaugh. Maybe you and I are more alike than I thought. Better yet, maybe you and Brett Kavanaugh are more alike than I thought."

O'Reilly chuckled.

"Not even close," said Cavanaugh. "Not even close."

"You mean to tell me you never put your hand over a young lady's mouth before like Kavanaugh had? You know, like, maybe when you were a teenager or something, and you didn't want her folks to hear nothing upstairs?"

"No, O'Reilly. I never have." Cavanaugh had heard enough.

"Say, listen—do you want to know what I told her?"

"Her? Who are you talking about? Who's her?"

"My little girl. Do you want to know what I told her about Kavanaugh—about *Brett* Kavanaugh?"

"I'm afraid to ask."

"I told her that he's a great man. I told her that he's a great man, a good father, and a good husband. I told her that he's got two daughters of his own and that he loves them more than anything else in this world. I told her that he's a Supreme Court judge. I told her that he's the best Supreme Court judge. I told her that he's a fair Supreme Court judge. And that's all I told her. And you know what she said to me then?"

Cavanaugh sighed into the phone, but O'Reilly went on regardless.

"'If only there were more people in this world like Brett Kavanaugh'—that's what she told me. That because what I said what I said to her about him, that she now loves her Brett Kavanaugh bobblehead—her 'Brett doll' is what she calls it—that much more, bobbly head and all. So, what do you say to that, huh, Cavanaugh? What do you say to that? Can you say that about yourself to your own daughter, Cavanaugh? Or to your wife—what's her name again?— Missus Cavanaugh? Can you say such things about yourself the way I did to my daughter about Brett Kavanaugh?"

Cavanaugh's mind was swimming for the right reply. It was so late, he was so tired, it felt as though he had all but forgotten how to talk.

"You can't, can ya?" said O'Reilly. "You can't say such things about yourself to your own wife and daughter because when it comes right down to it, you might be a Cavanaugh, Cavanaugh, but you ain't no *Brett* Kavanaugh and you never *will* be Brett Kavanaugh."

"I'll drink to that," said the voice. Or was that his own voice? Cavanaugh could no longer tell the difference.

"Whatever you say, O'Reilly. Whatever you say."

"Damn right whatever. Hey, that pitch from Kavanaugh—you have to admit, that sure was something, wasn't it? A perfect slider."

"Yeah, it sure was *something*, alright."

"It sure as hell was."

"Well, alright, O'Reilly. Is there anything else you have to say to me?"

"Yeah, a couple of things. First of all, who won the ballgame? I was nodding out so much at the end there that I can't even fucking remember."

Cavanaugh was about to fill his neighbor in on which team won, but before he could even open his mouth, O'Reilly was already on to the next thing.

"But also, there's the issue of my wife."

Here it was. It was what Cavanaugh had feared all along. He wished he had never called. But he knew he had to hear his neighbor out, if only because it might impact others more innocent.

"Your wife? What about your wife?"

"Well, you see, she's given me only one week to get out. One god-damn week is all she's given me. Says she's had it with all my boozing and sleeping around."

Cavanaugh was relieved to hear this. No one had been killed, and it sounded like no one was going to be killed either. He could hear O'Reilly's voice begin to crack, and then the weeping began.

"Oh, what am I going to do, Cavanaugh? What am I going to do? Without my wife. Without my little girl. Oh, what am I going to do?"

Cavanaugh let him sob it out for several seconds before offering his reply. "I don't know, O'Reilly. Maybe you can write a letter to your friend, Brett Kavanaugh. I'm sure he's found himself in that sort of situation as well. Maybe he can help."

"Well, that's a—hey, that's a pretty good idea, Cavanaugh. Maybe I'll take you up on that."

"Yeah, sure. Or maybe you can just go ask your daughter's Brett doll—maybe he can give you a couple of pointers as well."

"Oh, that's real funny, Cavanaugh. That's real fucking fun—"

Cavanaugh hung up the phone. He walked to the refrigerator, opened the door, and searched for something that was once always there for him but no longer.

"I could use a drink," he whispered.

CAVANAUGH BEGINS TO BOBBLE

CAVANAUGH WOKE UP with the early morning sunlight shining through the window.

"Here he is, Mommy," said Cavanaugh's daughter.

"Cavanaugh's daughter," said the voice.

"Cavanaugh's daughter," said Cavanaugh.

"*What?*" said Cavanaugh's daughter. "Did you just say Cavanaugh's daughter?"

Cavanaugh could no longer see his daughter's first name in his head the way he used to when he used to pick her up in his arms and give her shoulder rides. Her frame was still somewhat small, but she was growing rapidly now, and his aching back could not keep up.

"Sorry, honey. I, um, meant to say—"

"That's weird, Daddy. To call me *that*? Really, really weird."

"What's going on in here? What did he call you?" It was Mrs. Cavanaugh. She was dressed in a blouse and suit, ready for a full day at the office. His daughter was dressed as well, in a sweatshirt and dungarees, all set for school.

Cavanaugh looked about the couch from where he lay. It was only then that he finally realized that he was in the den, still in his undershirt and boxers.

How did I end up here? Cavanaugh wondered. He had no recollection of ever entering the room.

"What's the matter, Cavanaugh? Had trouble sleeping?" Mrs. Cavanaugh crouched down and brushed off the crumbs on Cavanaugh's chest with her hand. "Looks like someone had the munchies last night."

"Daddy called me Cavanaugh's daughter."

"Cavanaugh's daughter? Why did you call her Cavanaugh's daughter, Cavanaugh?"

Cavanaugh looked at Cavanaugh's daughter, then at Mrs. Cavanaugh. "Well, I didn't really mean—"

"Daddy, your penis. It's sticking out of your boxers. Not cool—right, Mommy?"

Mrs. Cavanaugh gasped, then quickly grabbed one of the pillows off the couch to cover up her husband.

"Relax, Mommy. It's just a penis. Right, Daddy?"

How a young child can be so innocent about certain things and so blunt about others at the same time always fascinated Cavanaugh.

He nodded his head. "And now the pillow has penis cooties," said Cavanaugh.

Cavanaugh's daughter giggled and left the room.

Mrs. Cavanaugh shook her head and twisted her husband's ear.

"Ow," said Cavanaugh, though it hurt less than his exclamation suggested.

"Listen, I love your penis, honey," said Mrs. Cavanaugh, "but you should keep yourself covered when she's around and get yourself dressed. Besides, don't you have a job to get to?"

"I suppose," said Cavanaugh.

Cavanaugh slid his fingers along Mrs. Cavanaugh's blouse. It was his favorite of all her blouses because it was made of satin.

Cavanaugh loved satin.

His hand was making its way along her chest when his daughter walked back into the room, cradling her Brett Kavanaugh bobblehead in her small arms.

Cavanaugh pulled his hand off his wife's bosom and pointed at the bobblehead. "What are you doing with that?"

"What do you mean what am I doing with it?" said Cavanaugh's daughter. "I'm bringing it to school."

"What for?"

"For show-and-tell. It's Thursday. We always have show-and-tell on Thursday."

"Honey, I don't think it's a good idea."

"Aw, why not, Cavanaugh?" said Mrs. Cavanaugh.

"Yeah, Daddy. Why not?"

"Because, um . . ." Cavanaugh was not sure what to say. "Well, um, what are you going to tell your classmates about it?"

"What do you mean what am I going to tell them?"

"You know, Cavanaugh," said Mrs. Cavanaugh, "you're acting really strange this morning."

"I'm just going to show it to them and tell them I got it at the game last night," said Cavanaugh's daughter. "Just going to show them how its head bobbles."

"That's all though, right?" said Cavanaugh.

"Hey, Mommy. Check this out." Cavanaugh's daughter pressed the button on the base of the bobblehead, and the oversized head of the little Brett Kavanaugh began to bobble frenetically, up and down, up and down, just like O'Reilly said it would. Cavanaugh's daughter then did her best impression of a bobbling bobblehead, and Mrs. Cavanaugh followed suit.

The two burst into laughter.

"Pretty funny, right?" said Cavanaugh's daughter.

"Be careful though, honey," said Cavanaugh.

"Careful about what?"

"Yeah, careful about what, Cavanaugh?" said Mrs. Cavanaugh.

"Be careful about . . ." Cavanaugh latched onto the first words he could think of. "Be careful about breaking it. Because if you break it, you know, we can't replace it, I mean."

But, oh, if she could only break it. Perhaps her bringing it to school will turn out for the best, thought Cavanaugh. At least it will get that damn doll out of the house.

"You're so negative, Cavanaugh," said Mrs. Cavanaugh.

"Look, I'm just saying."

"Don't worry, Daddy," said Cavanaugh's daughter. "I'll be careful with it." The young girl kissed Cavanaugh on the cheek, then hugged him. She was still his little angel, no matter how her name appeared inside his head.

"Besides," said Cavanaugh's daughter, "when they ask me who got it for me, I'm going to tell them it was you and tell them that you're the best daddy in the world."

"Aw, shucks, sweetie," said Cavanaugh. He kissed his little angel on the forehead.

Outside, something rumbled down the road. It was Cavanaugh's daughter's school bus, screeching to a stop near the corner. She grabbed her knapsack and ran toward the front door.

"So, long, pumpkin," said Mrs. Cavanaugh.

Both Cavanaugh and Mrs. Cavanaugh watched their daughter exit the house, with the latter continuing to observe through the window until the big, yellow bus pulled away. When it was out of sight, Mrs. Cavanaugh turned back to Cavanaugh and spoke first.

"So, you didn't really answer my question."

"Huh? What question are you talking about?" said Cavanaugh.

"The question I asked last night: What has gotten into you?"

Cavanaugh ran the back of his hand against the satin sleeve of his wife's arm, then along her cheek, his fingers edging closer to her mouth. He could still hear O'Reilly's voice ringing in his ears.

You mean to tell me you never put your hand over a young lady's mouth before like Kavanaugh had?

Cavanaugh quickly pulled his hand away, his fingers retrenching back down the slope of his wife's neck, toward her blouse again. He tried as best he could to cast aside the remarks from O'Reilly that were still lingering in his head, but even with Mrs. Cavanaugh's satin blouse at his fingertips, it was still a challenge.

"Cavanaugh, are you there? Are you going to answer my question, or what?" Mrs. Cavanaugh was waiting with anticipation.

"The question, Missus Cavanaugh—*Missus Cavanaugh? Did I just really say Missus Cavanaugh to her?*—is not what's gotten into *me*, the question is what's going to get into *you*."

"Oh, I, uh, kind of like that question, Cavanaugh," said Mrs. Cavanaugh, her frown transforming into a mischievous grin across the terrain of her fair-skinned and pockmarked face. "I can give you ten minutes. Ten minutes, and not a minute more."

Cavanaugh felt his love-shaft quickly harden inside his boxers, and, moments later, its head began to bobble. He finished up well-under Mrs. Cavanaugh's time limit.

Cavanaugh's Daughter Rides the School Bus

Cavanaugh's daughter saw two identical faces rise simultaneously above the back of the seat in front of her, their faces lightly freckled, square-jawed, and just shy of feminine.

"Who's that supposed to be?" the two faces said in unison.

The two identical faces belonged to a pair of pony-tailed identical sisters three years her senior who were known as the Tomboy Twins—that was the moniker handed down to them by the other children on the bus—and they were so in sync with one another, in movement and in language, that Cavanaugh's daughter, at times, had wondered if they were in fact still conjoined at the shoulder as they had been at birth, as one particular school-wide rumor suggested. For Cavanaugh's daughter, the fact that their shoulders were obstructed by the back of the bus seat over which they now peered down from only reinforced the potential veracity of that rumor.

"It's a bobblehead," she replied.

"Duh," they said together. "We know it's a bobblehead, but who's that bobblehead supposed to be?"

"Some guy who used to play baseball, I think, but doesn't anymore."

"You *think*?" said one of the twins.

"Uh-huh. I mean, I think he's too old to play now, but he did throw the ceremonial first pitch at the game last night. My dad said it was a perfect slider, whatever that means."

"You know," said the other twin, "his face sort of looks familiar. What's his name?"

"Brett Cavanaugh."

The two twins looked at one another, their eyeballs popping outward from their little sockets, their mouths resembling the shape of the letter O.

They turned back toward Cavanaugh's daughter.

"Did you just say Brett Kavanaugh?"

"Uh-huh. Why? What's wrong?"

"You mean, Brett Kavanaugh, the Supreme Court judge?"

"Yeah. Come to think of it, I think that's what the announcer said when he came out to the mound. Like he was a baseball player a long time ago, but now he's a judge or something, right?"

The two twins turned to one another, then broke into laughter in unison.

"What's so funny?" said Cavanaugh's daughter.

"I'm sorry," said one of the twins, "but did you just say that Brett Kavanaugh was a baseball player?"

"Well, yeah," said Cavanaugh's daughter. "I mean, wasn't he? Wasn't he a pitcher or something?"

The twins broke into laughter again, their matching braces stuck with the very same moist bits of breakfast cereal.

"What?" shouted Cavanaugh's daughter. "Why are you laughing? What in the world is so funny?"

The twins sank down behind the back of their seats in unison, but Cavanaugh's daughter could still hear their muffled giggling. A stocky, blonde-haired boy seated across from her shook his head.

"Don't pay any attention to them," said the boy. "They're just a couple of dykes."

"What's a dyke?" said Cavanaugh's daughter.

The boy rolled his eyes, shook his head again, then looked away.

Cavanaugh's daughter gazed out the window, and leaned her head against the glass, her head thumping to the rhythm of the bus. She felt embarrassed, but for what, she was not exactly certain. She did not speak or turn her head from the window for the rest of the ride.

The bus went uphill, then downhill, then back up the hill again. When it reached the school, and the children jumped out into the aisle to scramble off the bus, one of the Tomboy Twins poked her head from around the back of the seat. She smirked at Cavanaugh's daughter, and handed her a carefully folded sheet of loose-leaf paper.

Cavanaugh's daughter unfolded the sheet of paper and tried to read the five-word note as best she could, for she had only begun to learn how to read the previous school year. She was able to make out the first four words, but was unfamiliar with the last.

Brett Kavanaugh is a rapist, the note read.

Guess I'll have to look that last word up later, she figured. But was his last name actually Kavanaugh, and not Cavanaugh?

She wondered if her father knew about the difference in spelling.

She folded the note back to its original place, stuffed it in her knapsack, and rose from her seat. The bus driver, a genial-looking man who appeared to be a few years younger than her father, watched her through the rearview mirror as she walked down the aisle. When she passed by him at the front of the bus, he nodded and tipped his cap at her. This made her think of the man who was more than a few years older than her father—the one who tipped his cap after delivering a perfect slider.

"Just like Brett Kavanaugh," said a voice inside her head, but she mistook it for the voice of the bus driver.

"Did you just say something?" said Cavanaugh's daughter.

"I said have a nice day," said the bus driver.

"Oh," said Cavanaugh's daughter. "Thanks." She nodded back. "You, too." She looked over her shoulder at the empty aisle behind her, then back at the descending steps in front of her.

As always, she was the last child off the bus.

CAVANAUGH'S IS CAVANAUGH'S

CAVANAUGH WAS A PENCIL-PUSHER with a desk, a computer, a phone, and no pencils. His office was a cubicle within a small room, with neither a light switch nor window. Nor did his office have a clock, but Cavanaugh was not fond of clocks, or watches for that matter, for he feared things that ticked.

Despite having arrived at work a few minutes late after his quick morning rendezvous with Mrs. Cavanaugh, Cavanaugh was, he knew, unlikely to face any repercussions for his tardiness, for neither his co-workers nor his supervisor ever seemed to take note of his presence. He had, in general, ambivalent feelings about this lack of attention at his place of work, but he believed on a day such as this in which he felt lethargic and unfocused, it served him well.

Perhaps O'Reilly was right about the Kavanaugh doll, thought Cavanaugh. Maybe I'm making way too much of it.

But then there was the rest of what he had said that was still nagging at Cavanaugh, for reasons still not fully known to him.

Hey, man, haven't you ever done something like that to a girl, or, I mean, a woman before?

Done something like what?

You know, like, not like rape maybe, but maybe gone a little further than you should've?

The phone rang. It came as a relief to Cavanaugh to hear it ring. Anything to distract him from his thoughts.

Cavanaugh only used a landline phone at work. He was never a big fan of using those wireless earpods the rest of his colleagues swore by. Then again, he was not a frequent recipient of business calls, or any type of calls, for that matter. Like the lack of attention from his colleagues, this lack of inbound calls seemed to cut both ways in Cavanaugh's mind: though it might have meant less commissions for him, it also had allowed his mind more room to think.

Cavanaugh picked up the phone after the second ring.

"Hello, this is Cavanaugh."

"Oh, hi, Mister Cavanaugh. I was trying to reach Missus Cavanaugh earlier on her cell, but I guess she was unavailable. This is Missus—*oh fuck me Cavanaugh, fuck me Cavanaugh, fuck me*—your daughter's teacher."

Daughter's teacher?

"Is everything all right with my daughter?" said Cavanaugh. It came out more intensely than he intended, but then he figured if his daughter had been shot down at school like the rest of the kids on the news, this probably was not going to be the way that sort of message would be delivered.

"Oh, yes, everything's fine with her—she's totally all right," said his daughter's teacher.

What was his daughter's teacher's name again? He had not quite caught what she had said. He did not want to come off sounding like a disinterested father, so he decided against asking her to repeat it.

"Everything is fine," said the teacher. "Nothing to be alarmed about. It's just that—well, I don't know if you know this, but every Thursday here we have our show-and-tell in the morning—*Well, I actually do know, Missus . . . Missus—Do you like that when I do that to you, Missus Cavanaugh? Do you like it? Do you? Do you?*—she showed us her new doll—you know, the bobblehead? She says she got it from you as a gift—is that correct?"

"Excuse me, what was that you said?"

"I said the bobblehead doll. The Brett Kavanaugh bobblehead doll? I have to say, she really loves that doll. And watching his head bobble—well, your daughter's laugh is just so infectious, it made all her classmates laugh as well. It was sort of surreal, you know, seeing all my students—especially the female ones—getting so into that doll, pressing its button, passing it around. Just surreal."

"Yeah, well, um, I guess I can imagine." Cavanaugh managed an abbreviated chuckle, even though he knew it was probably inappropriate.

JOSHUA KORNREICH

"She said that you bought it for her last night at the baseball game you took her to with the girl from the other classroom—oh, what's that girl's name again?—it escapes me now, but she says you took her to the game last night and bought her the doll. Is that true?"

Cavanaugh knew what was coming.

I could use a drink.

"Yes," said Cavanaugh. "That is true."

"Ah. Well, you know, I don't usually do too much censoring of what my students bring into class—it's been my practice to leave that responsibility to their parents, which has worked out pretty well over the years, I have to say—but it has always been one of my guidelines for the parents to make sure that their child does not bring in anything that might offend or be politically or . . ."

"Of course, I—"

". . . morally sensitive."

"Right, I know. I—"

"So, her bringing in that Brett Kavanaugh doll—well, I don't think that was such a good idea."

"Oh, I totally agree, totally agree. I—"

"You see, Mister Cavanaugh, one of the other girls in the class came up to me as the students were lining up for lunch break, and asked if the doll was Brett Kavanaugh. She wanted to know, she said, because her mother told her that he did some bad things to women, so I told her that the doll was not *that* Brett Kavanaugh, but just some baseball player with a similar name, since, you know, I didn't want to traumatize her. Or me, for that matter."

"Well, I could totally understand that, and—"

"Mister Cavanaugh . . . If you don't mind me asking, what in the world were you thinking when you bought your daughter that doll?"

I could use a drink, I could use a drink, I could use a drink, I could use a drink.

"Well," said Cavanaugh, "I didn't want to buy it at first, but O'Reilly—*O'Reilly? Did I just say O'Reilly to her?*—he had already bought one for his daughter, and—and—"

"And?"

"And, well, I didn't want my daughter to feel sad about not getting one as well, so I bought one for her, but I never told her who he really was. O'Reilly—*said it again!*—he did that, he told his daughter all about Brett Kavanaugh and who he was, but I didn't ever tell *my* daughter who Brett Kavanaugh was, Missus—Missus—"

"But it was *your* daughter, Mister Cavanaugh, *your* daughter who brought a Brett Kavanaugh bobblehead into the classroom for show-and-tell, not Mister O'Reilly's daughter, correct?"

"Correct, but—"

"It was *your* daughter, Mister Cavanaugh. And I hope, for your daughter's sake, she never finds out who that doll really is, that he's not some retired baseball player, but a despicable human being. A drunk, a misogynist, a rapist, a sociopath, a con artist, a low-life, a scum-sucking—"

Cavanaugh hung up the phone. She was right, but he could no longer listen.

I could use a drink.

That voice again. It was back and was here to stay. And it was thirsty.

Cavanaugh looked back over one shoulder, then the other, to see if anyone was watching him, but of course no one was.

And how could they watch him? A cubicle stuffed inside an office room inside an office suite inside an office building inside an office plaza—how would anyone be able to watch him through all that?

Cavanaugh stood up from his swivel chair and reached under his neck to undo his necktie, but then remembered he had left his necktie at home.

He grabbed his empty briefcase—sometimes there were a few old receipts or periodicals inside his briefcase, but not today—and headed out the door. He left the clap-on lights on inside his office room so as not to attract attention to his early exit, though he knew such a measure was hardly necessary.

No attention was ever attracted when it came to Cavanaugh.

After all, Cavanaugh was just a Cavanaugh—not some Kavanaugh with a slick slider that made people take notice, that made people cheer, that made folks want to make bobblehead dolls out of him.

And even if there had been folks that wanted to make a bobble-head doll out of him, no one was ever going bring it to class for show-and-tell.

There was nothing to show when it came to Cavanaugh. There was nothing to tell.

Outside, there were no signs of co-workers or pedestrians. Cavanaugh took a big, deep breath of the crisp pre-autumn air around him, then blew out. It was now the middle of the afternoon.

Cavanaugh was not one to drive a car to and from work—he was a bus person. He walked to the bus station and boarded the first bus that arrived. It was not the usual one that brought him home. He found a seat toward the back, next to a window.

With his face leaning against the window, and his head tapping gently against the glass, Cavanaugh took note of the unfamiliar houses, shops, restaurants, and street names, as the bus chugged along its sinuous route, uphill, then downhill, then back up the hill again.

He waited for the sixth stop—or perhaps it was the seventh, figured Cavanaugh—and got off the bus. On the other side of the street from the stop was a bar. Cavanaugh walked across the street, never minding to look both ways as he crossed. When he reached the bar, he pulled the handle on its front door, but the door would not budge.

Probably because it's the middle of the afternoon, thought Cavanaugh. He would have to wait.

And so, too, would the voice have to wait.

"I could use a drink," it grunted.

Cavanaugh walked back across the street to the bus stop. He boarded the first bus that arrived and rode it for several stops, figuring that he would stay on it and kill some time until bars everywhere opened for happy hour rather than go home first.

Going home is not part of the plan, thought Cavanaugh.

He waited for stop after stop until he finally chose to disembark. When he got off at the bus stop of his choice, it was already starting to get dark outside.

Across the street from the stop was a bar. As he walked toward the bar, he suddenly realized it was the same bar as the bar he had tried to enter earlier, only this time, now that it was nighttime, he noticed the glow of the sign above its door, the neon letters all lit up.

CAVANAUGH'S, read the sign.

Cavanaugh nodded his head. He reached for the door and pulled. The bar was all his.

Cavanaugh Loves Jesus and Satan
and Mrs. Cavanaugh

I'll have another, thank you. Yeah, I'll hav a nutter, tanks. I sed ahl haf an udder, ank u. Hay ar yu def aw sumthin? Wot eye sed wuz gimmee uh fuk inn utter.

Kay.

Finely.

Jeesh.

Uh o.

Dats my fone.

Misses Cav a naw addit uh ghen.

Eye wuv Missis Cavawaw.

Wwwwwwwuv it wen shee wehrs dat sattin.

Hoo ee, eye luvvit.

Sheez gottis sattin blous, u c.

Cant git nuff uvvit.

Eye awww wayz say thairs ownlee too thins eye luhv mo dan jeezis: dats satan an Misses Cavunaw, u heer?

Dats awl.

Gotdat?

Oh yah, and mah widdle gurl.

Aw rite yall.

Wheh dat udda shot, ay?

Wheh fug izzit?

Diss plase—diss plase wuz naym faw mee.

Oh yay.

It wuz.

Itz cawl Cavunawz an datz my naym.

Naym faw me and itz my aw my.

Duh syne in frunt sez itz aw myna.

An ahm keeeepin it, u heer?

Awrite now, paw mee nutter shotter.

Paw mee nudder, gawdamyuh.

Gahd nose mee an dat dam voys insyde mee hed can yoos uh nuffer.

Tenks.

CAVANAUGH MEETS CAVANAUGH

A LOUD THUD awoke Cavanaugh from his bar stool. The first thing he saw was a gaunt, stone-faced man, older than he, standing on the other side of the counter. The man's eyes were bloodshot, his nose red and bulbous, his flannel checkered in white and green.

Cavanaugh turned his head and saw another man, one much heavier than the man behind the counter, dressed all in black, with knife-and-bone tattoos running up and down his arms and neck, a hoop-earring in either ear.

Must be the bouncer, figured Cavanaugh.

Inside one of the bouncer's pierced ears was a wireless earpod, just like the ones Cavanaugh's colleagues used at work.

"Sorry to wake you up from your nap," said the bouncer in a gruff voice.

"Wake me?" Cavanaugh looked around, not totally sure if the bouncer was addressing him or someone at the other end of the earpod.

The bar was empty. Cavanaugh could remember walking up to the counter, but could not remember anything after that.

"Yeah, wake you," said the bouncer. He gestured toward the man on the other side of the counter. "Mister Cavanaugh here has been waiting for you to wake up for the last hour. Says you were causing quite a stir in here earlier. Isn't that right, Mister Cavanaugh?"

The man behind the counter nodded. "That's right," he said. "This fella here was just sitting there, looking at me funny all night, giving me the ole hairy eyeball. I had already poured him several shots with him tossing his cash across the counter every time I poured him one. He kept hollering right in my face, demanding that I pour him another shot—'Pour me another, goddammit, pour me another,' he kept saying—but I could tell he had one too many as it was, so finally I said, 'No, I will not pour you another, sir,' and that's when this fella here started really ripping into me—maybe he thought I was someone else or something because then he got all up in my face again, barking like a dog, yelling, 'Fuck you, Brett, fuck you,' but my name isn't Brett, you see, it's Cavanaugh—that's my name, and I am the owner of this establishment—and I tried telling him all that, I tried telling him that my name is Cavanaugh and that I own this establishment, but this fella here, he wasn't having it, started moving his head up and down, up and down like some sort of crazy person, saying to me, 'No, you ain't fucking Cavanaugh—I'm fucking Cavanaugh, I'm fucking Cavanaugh,' and that's when folks started clearing out, thinking this guy was insane or something, and so that's when I called you in here from out front, but by the time you made it in here, this fella here had already fallen asleep right here on the stool here, his face flat down against the counter."

Cavanaugh listened to the man's story but could not recall the story or the man telling it. He studied the man behind the counter, then looked at the bouncer.

"Well?" said the bouncer, a stern expression on his face

"Well," said Cavanaugh, scratching his head, "I must've blacked out or something, because I can't recall a single thing he just said."

"Blacked out," said the voice inside his head. "Just like Brett Kavanaugh."

The bouncer rolled his eyes. "Blacked out, huh?"

"Yeah ... blacked out," said Cavanaugh. "But I *am* Cavanaugh, though. Really—I am. I mean, that's my name: Cavanaugh."

The bouncer grabbed Cavanaugh by the collar. "You ain't fucking Cavanaugh." He pointed to the stone-faced man behind the counter. "*He's* fucking Cavanaugh, and if you ain't out of this fucking bar by the time I count to five, I'm going to pick you right up off this stool here and fucking throw you out head first, ya hear?"

By the time Cavanaugh stumbled his way out of Cavanaugh's, the bouncer had only reached *three* in his count. Standing on the sidewalk, Cavanaugh felt a vibration inside the pocket of his pants.

It was his phone.

There were two new text messages from Mrs. Cavanaugh, asking where he was and what time he'll be home, plus a voice message with her name and phone number attached to it.

There was also another text message from O'Reilly: *heard about the big show and tell at school today lol*

Cavanaugh looked at the time on his phone. It was late, but not so late that he couldn't text Mrs. Cavanaugh to tell her that he had an emergency company meeting that was running overtime, and that, sorry, he could not have texted her in the middle of the meeting, and even if he could've texted her, there was lousy reception in the conference room anyway, so he wouldn't have been able to send or see any messages from her until later, which, he would say, *is* what had happened, of course.

Cavanaugh's head was pounding—not just from alcohol, but from guilt.

"Just like Brett Kavanaugh," said the voice again.

"I'm not like Brett Kavanaugh," said Cavanaugh to the voice. "I'm not anything like Brett Kavanaugh at all."

Cavanaugh smacked himself in the head a few times, hoping to jostle the voice out from where it dwelled, but the voice kept repeating the same thing over and over again during the entire bus ride back to his neighborhood: *Just like Brett Kavanaugh. Just like Brett Kavanaugh*—the very sound of the voice making Cavanaugh's head bobble up and down, up and down. The other passengers moved to the other side of the bus, away from him, as he continued to pummel away at his own bobbling head.

It was not until he stepped off the bus, just around the corner from his home, that something stopped Cavanaugh in his tracks, making him forget about the echoing voice inside his head: it was the O'Reilly house. All the lights were off inside it, except for a solitary glow from within one of the windows on the ground floor.

Cavanaugh thought about ignoring it altogether—the faster he got home, the less he would have to explain to his wife, he figured—

but the power of his curiosity overtook him, as he tiptoed to the window from which the glow was coming from.

When he reached the window, he could see that the glow was actually coming from a TV screen hanging on a wall in what appeared to be a family room of sorts. On the screen was a woman and a very young girl. They were smiling, laughing, doing many different things in many different settings—skipping, running, dancing, swimming, riding bicycles, playing hopscotch, building sandcastles, or sometimes just talking. Every now and then, the woman or the girl would point or wave directly at the camera filming them.

Cavanaugh could see part of O'Reilly's head as it tilted back again and again in front of the screen with each swig of his beer can. Cavanaugh thought he heard some sort of muttering, then a whimpering, coming from the TV that belied the joyful expressions of the girl and the woman on the screen. After listening in silence for a while, Cavanaugh realized that the woeful sounds were not coming from either of the females onscreen but rather from the man on the couch watching them.

There he was—O'Reilly—his broad head slouching forward into the glow before him, his large, trembling hands making shadows against the wall as he wept. Cavanaugh looked on as his neighbor shook, up and down, back and forth, hands now clenched into fists in front of him, beating uncontrollably against the cascading slope of forehead and face.

Cavanaugh had seen enough and was about to turn and leave when he suddenly caught a glimpse of his reflection in his neighbor's window. He studied it for a moment, but did not like what he saw.

"Just like O'Reilly," said the voice. "Just like O'Reilly."

Cavanaugh backed away from the window, his eyes tearing, his body shivering against the nighttime wind.

He lumbered back to the road and continued his way home, his head still heavy but no longer pounding.

Somewhere in the dark, a dog barked.

CAVANAUGH SEES A SHADOW

"YOU HAVEN'T been yourself lately."

Mrs. Cavanaugh said it loud, for Cavanaugh had marched right up the stairs when he returned home, and went right into the shower stall of their shared bathroom, knowing he had to remove any evidence of where he had been, including the stench of his person. He had grabbed the mouthwash from the medicine cabinet before entering the stall, and was swishing the mouthwash around in his mouth, as she spoke. They were inches away from each other, he and his wife, yet barely translucent to one another through the stall door.

"Especially since last night," Mrs. Cavanaugh continued. "It seems that ever since you returned from that baseball game, something about you has changed."

"Changed?" said Cavanaugh. "I've changed? What about me has changed?" Posing a question when being posed with one yourself is always a good strategy, thought Cavanaugh. Someone had told him that long ago—an old acquaintance from his college days perhaps. It was a strategy often deployed by his colleagues on one another among the cubicles at work.

As he awaited his wife's response, Cavanaugh continued on with his swishing. The steam of the shower felt good against his chafing skin and the bobbling symptoms his head had experienced earlier in the night had fully subsided.

"Well, the way you left our bedroom in the middle of the night last night and woke up in the den," said Mrs. Cavanaugh, "and then the way you were this morning—"

"What was wrong with the way I was this morning?"

Another question. The strategy was working—he could feel it.

"I mean, nothing was wrong, honey—I mean, I enjoyed it, you know, on the couch and all—but the way you were calling me Missus Cavanaugh, Missus Cavanaugh, over and over again, Missus Cavanaugh, Missus Cavanaugh—well, it was just a little, um . . . you know, um . . . strange."

"Missus Cavanaugh," said the voice inside Cavanaugh's head. "Just like your mother."

A chill went up Cavanaugh's back. Perhaps it was just the alcohol working its way out of his body.

He took a deep breath. "Yes, I suppose it was strange." Cavanaugh watched the mouthwash swirl around his feet and trickle down the drain.

The translucent figure on the other side of the stall continued: "And the way you were even before that. You know, with the doll?"

"What about the doll?" Cavanaugh sounded more cross than he intended, but he feared where this was going.

"I don't know—I mean, you seemed so flustered about her bringing it to school today. Didn't quite understand what the big deal about it was."

Cavanaugh thought about telling Mrs. Cavanaugh about the phone call he had received from their daughter's teacher but decided against it. He figured that conversation could go in a lot of different directions, none of them good for him.

"You're right, honey." Cavanaugh opened the stall door, and Mrs. Cavanaugh was staring right at him, in her night robe.

The night robe was not the satin one that he liked, but a polyester one.

"Maybe I just need a good night's sleep," said Cavanaugh, toweling off. "Or maybe it's work. I don't know."

"You know, I left you dinner downstairs," said Mrs. Cavanaugh. "It's probably gotten cold by now."

Cavanaugh was not exactly hungry, in no small part due to the unknown yet undoubtedly large quantity of alcohol he had just consumed. Just the thought of eating made Cavanaugh want to hurl. But he did not wish to upset Mrs. Cavanaugh over her generous efforts, so he kissed her cheek.

"Thanks, love," said Cavanaugh.

He quickly changed into his usual nightwear—an undershirt and boxers—and made his way out of the bedroom. Relief swept over him as he made his exit, as well as the feeling as though he had gotten away with something.

I won't ever drink again, he promised himself. I mean it.

Down the hallway, the door to his daughter's bedroom had been left ajar, and he could tell that the lights inside the room were still on. He knocked on the door and poked his head in.

"Hey, angel," said Cavanaugh. "How was school today?"

Cavanaugh's daughter was sitting at her desk, her glasses covering her eyes. She looked up from her sticker album. "Good," she said. "I guess." She seemed unsure of her response. She twirled a strand of her red hair with her finger.

Cavanaugh pretended not to notice. Tonight was not the night to engage. He looked over at her nightstand. The Brett Kavanaugh bobblehead was back in its position, watching over her bed.

Cavanaugh's daughter followed his gaze, then looked back at him. "Is everything all right, Daddy?"

"All right?" The question made Cavanaugh wonder how much of his earlier inebriety was still evident. Or perhaps she was simply just deploying the very same strategy he had used on her mother. She was, after all, a Cavanaugh, and thus probably had a god-given ability to be cunning when necessary. "Well, what do you mean by all right?"

"I don't know," said Cavanaugh's daughter. She shrugged her shoulders.

"Don't know?" Cavanaugh wondered: Was she just being coy with him?

She sighed. "I guess what I mean is was there something you wanted to tell me?"

Cavanaugh paused for a moment. There *was* something he wanted to tell her, but he was not ready to tell her what that something was.

"There is nothing I need to tell you, sweetie. Just checking in. I'm going to go downstairs and see what Mommy left in the kitchen for me. I'll say goodnight now."

He leaned over and kissed her forehead. She squeezed him tight, as if she did not want him to leave just yet, but leave he did.

When he closed her bedroom door behind him, the voice inside his head spoke: "She already knows."

"Knows?" muttered Cavanaugh as he entered back into the hallway. "Knows about what?"

"About me," said the voice. "About me, Brett Kavanaugh."

"No, no," muttered Cavanaugh to himself. "There's no way. She can't know." He was about to smack his head again, but then caught his reflection in the hallway mirror.

He thought of the window at O'Reilly's house, and remembered what his neighbor looked like, just sitting there on the couch, pounding away at his own head.

"Just like O'Reilly," said the voice. "Just like O'Reilly."

Cavanaugh thudded down the stairs and lumbered into the kitchen. There it was, on the table, waiting for him: a plate of microwaved meat lasagna. He grabbed the plate off the table, as well as the fork sitting next to it, and took a whiff.

The aroma alone was enough to bring some of his usual appetite right back to him. He took a couple of quick bites, as he stood alone in the middle of the kitchen. The pasta was cold in some spots, but the meat was still somewhat warm. He ate half of what was on the plate and scraped what remained of the meat lasagna into the kitchen trash bag. He tied the top of the bag into a knot, walked out the front door of the house, marched down the driveway, and tossed the bag into the garbage bin.

Cavanaugh did not mind the more-than-remote possibility of his neighbors seeing him with only his undershirt and boxers on.

Something about you has changed.

Cavanaugh made it halfway back to his front door, when he suddenly felt something surge in his gut. He turned and scrambled back down the driveway, and heaved out from his mouth whatever evidence remained of his after-work adventure into the garbage bin.

That, along with the few bites or so of the meat lasagna, of course.

When he finished, he looked down at his undershirt. It was covered in vomit.

Cavanaugh removed his undershirt and tossed it into the bin with the rest of the evidence. He was now outside, in the dark, with only his boxers to cover him.

Somewhere down the block, a dog barked—the same dog that barked on his way home, Cavanaugh figured, but there was no real way of telling: the neighborhood was overrun with dogs. Cats, too, he imagined. Cavanaugh had never been given the opportunity to enter any of the houses of his neighbors to confirm such a conjecture, however, for the only house he had ever entered in his neighborhood was his own.

Across the street, a light flickered on through one of the top-floor windows, the shade behind it rising upward. Cavanaugh could see a shadow of a figure through the window, but could not decipher if the figure was that of a man or a woman.

Too many shadows tonight, thought Cavanaugh. The neighborhood is overrun with *them* as well.

The shadow across the street seemed to be watching Cavanaugh, as the latter stood underneath the lamppost at the foot of his front lawn.

Cavanaugh waved at the shadow, but the shadow did not wave back. He waved again, but the shadow remained still.

Perhaps it's a figment of my imagination, thought Cavanaugh. Or perhaps it's just an unfriendly shadow.

"Or perhaps I could use a drink," said the voice inside his head.

"Yeah, yeah, right," said Cavanaugh. He turned back around and surveyed his own house. Every light was now off.

They're already sound asleep, he figured.

"Everyone except the Brett Kavanaugh doll," said the voice.

Cavanaugh walked back up the driveway, toward his house. He looked back over his shoulder one more time, toward the house across the street.

The shadow was gone, and so was the light surrounding it, the window shade having been pulled back down.

Upon reentering his house, Cavanaugh shut the door behind him, and slowly tiptoed up the stairs. The sound of snoring grew louder with every step.

When Cavanaugh entered the master bedroom, the snoring came to an end.

Mrs. Cavanaugh gargled up some phlegm, then spoke: "How was the meat lasagna, Cavanaugh?"

CAVANAUGH RUNS UP THE STAIRS

WHAT HE SAW confused his young boy eyes at first—the two of them on the couch in the living room, one on top of the other—the shadow on top, her on the bottom—her wrists held down against the support of the couch, then the seat of the couch, the shadow covering more and more of her slender figure as she tried to push back up. She shifted about underneath the shadow, trying to wriggle herself free, her barrette dangling loose from her flowing brown hair, a strap of her dress slipping down off her shoulder, the cream-white of her brassiere exposed.

"No, no," she said.

"Shh, shh," the shadow said.

The boy did not know who the shadow was, but knew it was a shadow he had seen before. Still, he was too scared of the shadow to even budge.

"Stop, stop," she said, swinging her face back and forth.

"Missus Cavanaugh, Missus Cavanaugh," the shadow said, as if attempting to calm her.

"I'm not your missus," she said. "I'm not your missus no more."

"You *are* my missus," the shadow said. "You'll always be my missus, no matter what."

The shadow was no longer a shadow now, but a man, his pasty and pockmarked cheekbones spasming above her face in an ecstatic fit of rage, yet still trying to calm the woman underneath him, to soothe her as she screeched, his face in her face, a smirk forming now across his lips, pushing himself down on her, a hand now over her mouth to stop her mouth from screaming, from telling him to stop, from telling the boy—*her* boy—to leave, to look away, to leave, to go upstairs, to leave, Mom's alright, leave, go, upstairs, now.

"Easy, Missus Cavanaugh," said the man on top of her. "Easy now. Easy."

Up the stairs the boy ran, to his bedroom, and though he could no longer hear his mother as he lay curled up on his bed, he could still hear the sounds of the man on top of his mother coming from downstairs.

A moan—that was what he could hear.

A moan, then another moan, then another—all from the man who was on top of his mother.

The moans culminated in a great, thunderous shaking—a vibration of furniture, perhaps—and then a silence. The boy knew the silence meant it had ended. But the silence was a brief silence, for out of that brief silence grew new sounds whose sources the young boy could identify without even having to see them for himself.

The jingle of belt against buckle.

The clank of boot against wood.

The creak of a front door swung open.

The drone of the late afternoon air.

The barking from a dog down the road—as if the very opening of the door itself was what made the dog bark, thought the young boy, his head half-buried into the pillow on his bed.

But with a good, hard slam of the door, all the sounds—the jingling, the clanking, the creaking, the drone of the air, the barking from the dog—came to an end, leaving nothing for the boy to listen to except for the interior sounds of a house he shared with no one save his mother.

"I should have protected her," whimpered the young boy.

"You should have protected her," whispered the voice inside the young boy's head.

Somewhere downstairs, a clock ticked.

Somewhere downstairs, a refrigerator hummed.

Somewhere downstairs, a tea kettle whistled.

Somewhere downstairs, a woman wept in the dark.

CAVANAUGH THANKS GOD

CAVANAUGH WOKE UP with a mild hangover and without his wife in the bed next to him. The room, it seemed to him, was shaking ever so slightly.

He looked at the clock radio on Mrs. Cavanaugh's nightstand. It was already two hours into the workday.

"Fuck," said Cavanaugh. He shot up from his bed, and headed for the bathroom. He looked in the mirror of the medicine cabinet and studied his face.

Same old Cavanaugh, only with baggy and bloodshot eyes.

"What about your head?" said the voice.

The voice. It was still there.

"What about my head?" said Cavanaugh aloud to the empty bathroom.

"Take a closer look in the mirror, Cavanaugh," said the voice.

Cavanaugh moved his head closer to the mirror and took a good hard look.

"My head," said Cavanaugh. "It's twitching."

"It's more like a nodding, if you ask me," said the voice. "Ha! Like an old nodder, Cavanaugh—that's what you've become."

"Like a bobbling bobblehead," said Cavanaugh. "A bobbling bobblehead without a power button to turn it all off."

"All that head-bobbling," said the voice. "It's making me very dizzy in here."

Cavanaugh began to panic. "What am I going to do about it?"

"Relax, Cavanaugh," said the voice. "Perhaps no one will notice."

"But perhaps someone will," said Cavanaugh. He opened the cabinet, and took out two aspirin.

"Better make it three," said the voice.

Cavanaugh performed his usual bathroom routine and got dressed quickly. He was about to head downstairs when he decided to pay a visit to his daughter's bedroom.

No one was in the room—no one except for the Kavanaugh doll.

The doll was still sitting on the nightstand, but instead of watching over her bed, it was now smirking right at Cavanaugh as he entered the room. Cavanaugh sized the doll up for a bit, then lifted it off the nightstand to get a better look.

Its shiny, red cap.

Its merry, pink cheeks.

The smirk.

It really did look like Brett Kavanaugh. It would be only a matter of time until Mrs. Cavanaugh figured it out.

The doll could not stay.

Cavanaugh carried the doll out of the room and made his way down the stairs. There was no one waiting for him in the kitchen, but he could smell the scent of bread having been recently toasted. A box of cereal—the pebbled orange and grape one that was his daughter's favorite—stood upright on the table, its top left open.

He took a handful of what was inside the box and shoved it into his mouth.

Not bad, he thought.

With the Brett Kavanaugh bobblehead doll in one hand and his briefcase full of nothing in the other, he headed out the front door.

The sun was shining.

It was Friday, thank god.

Birds were chirping.

Somewhere down the road, a dog barked.

Missus Cavanaugh. Missus Cavanaugh.

Cavanaugh did not want to think about the past, his mother, the man he barely knew, the sounds the man and his mother made. It was too much for him to deal with in his head.

"I could use a drink," said the voice inside his head.

"No," Cavanaugh whispered. "Not now. Not ever again."

A bus arrived at the corner in short order.

Cavanaugh loved taking the bus. He owned a car and knew how to drive it, but, nevertheless, he did not drive it. When it came to driving, he let Mrs. Cavanaugh do all the driving.

The idea of driving was not something that Cavanaugh was fond of. There was, he felt, too much at stake out there on the open road, too many variables to weigh and consider.

On the bus, he recognized no one, not even the driver. He took a seat in the back and looked out the window. He thought about what he would tell his boss when he arrived so late for work, but knew, with a solid sense of certainty, that no one in his office was going to care or, for that matter, even notice.

He wondered if some of his co-workers even knew he worked there, buried in that cubicle inside an office room inside an office suite inside an office building inside an office plaza.

Besides, it was Friday. Who the fuck cared about anything on Friday?

Cavanaugh put his hand to his head. The twitching had all but subsided.

Stops were made, and some people got on the bus, and some people got off the bus. The bus rumbled its way uphill, then downhill, then back up the hill again. By the time the bus had reached Cavanaugh's stop, it was just Cavanaugh and the bus driver.

The bus driver announced the cross street on the intercom and waited. Cavanaugh did not move.

The bus driver announced the cross street again. Cavanaugh still did not move.

The bus driver turned and looked at Cavanaugh, as Cavanaugh continued to gaze out the window.

The bus driver drove on.

Cavanaugh waited a few more stops, then got off the bus. It was at a stop he was not familiar with, a bustling main street with restaurants, a drugstore, a grocery store, and a plaza complete with mini-mall and fountain.

He walked a block or two uptown, and found himself face-to-face with the front door of a bodega.

He read the sign above the door: MUST BE 21 OR OLDER TO BUY ALCOHOL.

He opened the door, and a steel bell above him jingled.

Belt against buckle.

Boot against wood.

He was about to grab a six-pack out of the bodega's see-through refrigerator, when he heard a voice. It was a voice not from inside his own head but from behind the glass of the bodega's sandwich counter.

"Can I help you?"

Cavanaugh could not see the person who greeted him. He could tell the voice was a voice of a man who sounded many years older than he himself was—and since Cavanaugh could not see this much-older man on the other side of the counter, he figured that this much-older man must also be much shorter as well.

"Thanks," said Cavanaugh, "but I think I'm okay here." He turned back toward the refrigerator and snatched the six-pack.

"Are you?" said the voice.

Cavanaugh turned to face the counter again and stood on his toes to get a better look of the man stationed behind it, but to no avail.

"Am I what?"

"Are you, in fact, okay?" The man's voice was a strong baritone that seemed to bounce and echo off the walls of the bodega.

"Well," said Cavanaugh, "I, um—I believe so."

"It's ten-thirty in the morning," said the voice.

"Yeah, well, I, uh, kind of know that already," said Cavanaugh.

"Ten-thirty in the morning," said the voice again. "Ten-thirty in the morning, and you want a six-pack—is that correct?"

Cavanaugh leaned his face into the see-through sandwich counter, but still could not see the man fully, only a translucent sense of him through the glass. He knew what the man behind the voice was getting at, but he made up his mind to refuse to acknowledge it.

"Well, you know," said Cavanaugh, "I'm saving it for later, of course."

"For later, eh?"

"Yup. For later."

"Alright then, young sir," said the voice behind the counter. "You can go help yourself at the front of the store there. It's self-checkout."

"Oh, um, that's great. Thanks a lot."

Cavanaugh walked toward the front of the store, his empty brief-case in one hand, his six-pack of beer in the other, and the doll tucked under his arm, but then he turned around. He got on his toes again, but he still could not see the face of the man behind the glass counter, nor make out his gray, translucent image any further.

Must've gone to the back, figured Cavanaugh.

He placed the bobblehead doll on the checkout counter, and then walked back toward the glass refrigerator again and opened the sliding door.

The air from the refrigerator felt good against his face. He snatched another six-pack, same brand, and headed back toward the front of the store.

He had just pulled a small extra paper bag from the self-checkout and placed it into his briefcase, when he heard the deep baritone voice boom out from behind the counter again.

"Say, that doll you got there—is that Brett Kavanaugh?"

Both the voice and the question took Cavanaugh by surprise, unsettled him.

"Um . . . yeah," said Cavanaugh. "That's him alright. Or a doll of him, anyway."

"Thought so," said the voice. "Hey, that was some pitch he threw the other night—did you see it?"

The voice seemed to come from not really behind the counter but beyond it, as if it were hovering over the entire bodega from somewhere up above.

"Well, actually," said Cavanaugh, "I was there, at the game. With my daughter."

"Your daughter? You brought your daughter to *that* game? On Brett Kavanaugh Night you brought her?"

"Well, I didn't know it was going to *be* Brett Kav—"

"Didn't know, did ya? How about your wife? What'd she have to say about it?"

Cavanaugh thought about asking the voice behind the counter how he even knew he had a wife, but then remembered the ring on his ring finger.

But how could the man even see the ring from where he was speaking?

Cavanaugh did not know what to say. "Well, I don't think she even knows the doll is supposed to be Brett Kavanaugh."

"Doesn't know?" said the voice. "Well, hell, how could that even be? It looks just like the guy."

"Um, yeah, well—"

"So, the doll—is it *your* doll or your daughter's doll?"

"The doll is . . ." Cavanaugh thought for a moment. "Well, um, I'm not really sure now whose doll it is. I mean, it *was* hers, but now it's—it's—it's—"

"Yours?"

"Um, yeah—I mean, I guess for the moment it is anyway." Cavanaugh chuckled uncomfortably at his own reply, wondering if he should have come up with a different one. Fearing the prospect of an awkward silence, he quickly decided to double down. "Yes. Yes, I suppose it *is* my doll."

"Well, it's a handsome-looking doll, your doll—that's for sure. Sure it makes for fine company. Got me quite a bobblehead collection going myself, yessir."

"Well, actually, I'm not a collector or anything. This one's my first."

"Well, I suppose there's a first for everything. Even when it comes to them bobbleheads."

There was a long pause. Cavanaugh stood there and waited. He was afraid to move.

The anonymous voice behind the counter spoke again: "Well, you go on ahead now and have a nice day."

"You too," said Cavanaugh.

"Be careful out there. Take good care of that doll."

Cavanaugh chuckled uncomfortably again. "Oh, I will."

With his briefcase in one hand, two brown paper bags full of beer in the other, and the Kavanaugh doll tucked under his arm, Cavanaugh took two small steps back toward the counter, hoping to finally catch a glimpse of the man bidding him farewell, but before he could even fully bring himself to take on such a fruitless endeavor, he turned back toward the front door, and quickly exited, the bell jingling from above.

Belt against buckle.

Boot against wood.

Outside, the voice from behind the bodega counter still lingered in his head.

Ten-thirty in the morning. Ten-thirty in the morning and you want a six-pack.

"Must be ten-thirty-five, ten-forty by now," muttered Cavanaugh.

"I could use a drink," said a voice. This time it was the one inside his head.

Cavanaugh walked back to the plaza that he had passed earlier, and found a bench across from the fountain. He sat down on the bench and pulled out the small paper bag from his briefcase, then snapped the briefcase shut. He then plucked one of the cans out from one of the six-packs, and placed it inside the paper bag, concealing it as he held it.

Cavanaugh looked to his left, to his right, then over his shoulder.

No one was watching.

No one cared.

No one ever cared when it came to Cavanaugh.

Be careful out there.

He cracked open the concealed can, took a large gulp, and waited for the water to rise.

Next to him on the bench, watching him as he drank, was the Brett Kavanaugh doll, its idle head bobbling ever so gently to the rhythm of the breeze.

Cavanaugh's head had already begun to bobble a bit again as well, but he paid it no notice.

"Thank god it's Friday," said Cavanaugh.

"Thank god it's Friday," echoed the voice.

O'REILLY GOES TO WORK

O'REILLY WOKE UP in the late morning and decided to be Cavanaugh. Whether the idea came to him in a dream or during his drinking binge from the night before, he was not certain, but when his eyes opened, and he found himself on the family room couch with the TV tuned to a blacked-out regional sports channel, the idea was sitting right there in his brain, ready and waiting for him.

He rose from the couch.

He limped up the stairs.

He peed.

He washed his hands.

He showered.

He combed his hair.

He put on fresh clothing: boxers, chinos, dress socks, and a button-down.

He went back downstairs to his empty kitchen.

He poured organic cereal and organic milk into a porcelain bowl, and then consumed everything in it.

He read the paper.

He belched.

He farted.

He farted again.

He went to the closet and grabbed the briefcase that Mrs. O'Reilly had given to him as a birthday present long ago, and which, up until now, had never been used.

With his smartphone in one hand and his briefcase full of nothing in the other, O'Reilly opened the front door, limped down his driveway, and headed up the sidewalk, as he made his way toward the bus stop.

He got on the bus when the bus came and took a seat next to the window.

He leaned his face against the window, his head tapping and thumping up against the glass, as the bus went uphill, then downhill, then back up the hill again.

When the bus driver announced Cavanaugh's stop, O'Reilly got off the bus and limped across the plaza toward Cavanaugh's office building.

Inside the building, no one noticed him, let alone his limp.

He took the first elevator he could up to Cavanaugh's floor, his phone still in one hand, the briefcase full of nothing still in the other.

The elevator dinged and the doors slid open.

He limped left.

He limped right.

He saw men.

He saw women.

Somewhere beyond the maze of cubicles, he spotted an office door with the name he had been looking for: CAVANAUGH.

He took a deep breath, then knocked.

CAVANAUGH MISSES HIS STOP

CAVANAUGH HAD JUST finished off his fourth can, when his phone vibrated inside his pocket.

It was O'Reilly. He had sent a selfie of himself, along with a text message: *guess where I am*

He took a closer look at the photo above the text. He could barely make out the nameplate in the background next to O'Reilly's oversized cranium, for the top half of it was offscreen, but there was no mistaking what the bottom half of the nameplate said: CAVANAUGH.

Cavanaugh looked back at O'Reilly's face, his eyes opened wide in the photo to exaggerated effect, his tongue unfurled from his mouth, his fingers in the formation of an anarchy sign.

Or was it a peace sign? Cavanaugh was not up on his finger signs as of late.

He was also unsure of why O'Reilly would be sitting in *his* office chair, at *his* desk, in *his* cubicle, in *his* office room. Or, better yet, how did he know where his office even was?

And why was he wearing a button-down dress shirt, and why was his hair so neatly combed for a change?

Cavanaugh put the remainder of his stash back in the bags, grabbed the bobblehead and his briefcase full of nothing, and walked briskly out of the plaza, past the grocery store, past the drugstore, past a couple of casual dining spots, until he made it back to the bus station, where, as Irish luck would have it, a bus awaited him. It was not until he stumbled into one of the seats in the back, that he realized that he was more than a little buzzed.

Still, he thought, I need to get to the office, for there was no telling what O'Reilly was up to.

He looked down at what was on his lap. But what about the beer?

Cavanaugh thought hard about this for a moment—perhaps going back to the office was not such a great idea after all, for how would he conceal the remaining beer cans?—but then quickly cast all worry aside, for he knew as long there was no chance anyone would ever take notice of him at the office, there was no chance anyone would ever take notice of anything he tried to smuggle into the office either.

No one ever took notice of anything when it came to Cavanaugh.

No one except for Mrs. Cavanaugh, of course.

Mrs. Cavanaugh always took notice when it came to anything about Cavanaugh.

What's gotten into you, Cavanaugh? You've been acting strange lately.

Gazing out the window of the bus, Cavanaugh thought about his wife and daughter, and wondered how he could ever face them again. He had not taken a single sip of alcohol since his daughter was born— that is, until these past couple of days.

The voice inside his head grew louder: "I could use a drink."

The voice still sometimes sounded like Brett Kavanaugh to Cavanaugh, but sometimes it sounded a bit different. While Cavanaugh could not quite put a finger on it, his other fingers were managing themselves just fine, as they finessed another can open. He looked around to see if anyone was looking, but it was only then that he realized that it was just he and the driver again who remained on the bus.

"Number five," said the voice.

Maybe the voice still sounded like Brett Kavanaugh after all, thought Cavanaugh.

"Yes, it *does* still sound like Brett Kavanaugh, indeed," said the voice. "A very *drunk* Brett Kavanaugh."

The bus managed to reach the stop where his office was located in reasonable time, but Cavanaugh had already made it halfway through number six when he dozed off in his seat, his head thudding against the window, beer dripping down the crotch of his pants, as the bus chugged along on its hilly and circuitous route.

When he woke up several minutes later, Cavanaugh recognized the sound immediately: a dog was barking. He could not see it, but it was coming from somewhere down the road.

"Sir, may I help you?"

Cavanaugh pulled his sweaty forehead from the window where it had grown stuck, and turned to the direction of the voice addressing him.

Whose voice was it?

"The bus driver's," said the voice inside his head.

Cavanaugh looked up at the bus driver, a bearded man with a kind yet concerned look on his face. "Oh, um, hey, bus driver—*bus driver?*—I think this is my stop."

"Well, I'm sure it is, sir, but it looks like you're going to need some help there getting off this bus."

"What time is it?"

"Not sure. My phone is up by the driver seat. Two-thirty, two forty-five, I imagine."

"Guess you don't like watches either, huh?"

The bus driver shook his head. "Too heavy on the wrist for my taste."

. . . her wrists held down against the support of the couch, then the seat of the couch, the shadow covering more and more of her slender figure as she tried to push back up . . .

"Easy now," said the bus driver, as he helped the drowsy, drunken passenger to his feet.

Cavanaugh held on tight to the bag full of beer in one hand and the briefcase full of nothing in the other, his head nodding, his neck twitching, as the bus driver led him to the exit at the front of the bus.

Easy, Missus Cavanaugh. Easy now. Easy.

"Wait," shouted Cavanaugh, as he spun around to where his seat had been. "Forgot something."

Cavanaugh hurried back to his seat and picked up the Kavanaugh doll. It was sitting upright, turned away from him, as if it were gazing out the window. As he looked down at the doll in his hands, he could see the puddle on the floor in front of the seat and took note of the wet spot on the lap of his trousers.

Had that come from the beer or from inside his pants?

He looked up from his wet lap and saw the bus driver standing at the center of the bus, staring right at him, arms folded, the look on his face having gone from kind to cross.

"Well, are you getting off this bus, or what?"

Cavanaugh hugged the doll against his chest with one hand, and held his bag of beer and briefcase full of nothing with the other, the latter item banging into the back of every seat, as he awkwardly made his way toward the front of the bus and down the exit steps unassisted. He had hardly gotten both feet on the pavement when the bus lurched off the curb, its fumes forming a cloud around Cavanaugh and his stash.

Somewhere down the road, a dog barked.

Was it the same dog?

Cavanaugh was not certain. He looked back and forth from house to house, yard to yard, looking for signs of the dog, but no matter how far he made it down the road, the barking seemed to come from the same distance, as if it were projecting from some fixed point inside his head.

Cavanaugh wondered: "*Is* it from inside my head?"

"Perhaps," said the voice.

"Ruff-ruff," said the dog.

By the time he reached his house—the red one, with black shutters around the windows—Cavanaugh had already made it through most of number seven.

Had anyone been watching?

Cavanaugh looked to his left, then to his right.

His shoulders moved up, then down. He was so shit-faced, he no longer cared.

He lifted the lid of the garbage bin at the foot of his driveway, and placed the few remaining beers underneath the trash bag inside. He thought about the barf-stained undershirt from the night before for a moment—he was not sure if it was still in the bin—and wondered if it had slipped down below, now making contact with his stash, but that thought quickly escaped him as he closed the lid and surveyed the house across the street.

The shades held still within their frames.

No sign of the shadow this time. It was the middle of the afternoon—perhaps it only came out at night.

Cavanaugh turned to face his house—the Cavanaugh house. No lights were on, but there were signs of life: he could smell smoke coming through the half-open kitchen window—toaster smoke, he figured—and the muffled sounds of voices unfamiliar, reverberating not from his head this time, he was certain, but from the TV inside the room the Cavanaughs called a den.

Cavanaugh peered through the window of the den, and watched his daughter watch. It was a cartoon with talking pigs. The pigs sounded British to Cavanaugh. Every now and then, his daughter would giggle, as she fidgeted about the couch.

Cavanaugh turned around and looked again at the house across the street.

One of the shades had moved.

A shadow appeared in the window frame.

He was being watched again.

Someone is watching me watching my daughter watch, thought Cavanaugh.

The thought made him dizzy.

Something tapped over his shoulder. He turned back toward his own house and saw his daughter, waving with one hand, rapping the window with her knuckles with the other, the reddish-brown freckles on her smiling face visible through the glass.

He could not hear her, but he was able to read her lips: *You brought home my bobblehead.* She rubbed her hands together, then clasped them under her chin, as she leaned against the window sill. She seemed to not even notice Cavanaugh at first, only the bobble-head.

Cavanaugh could see his reflection next to his daughter's face. It was a strange and tired face to Cavanaugh, the eyes baggy and bloodshot, the thinning hair atop his head disheveled, his head twitching and jerking about more noticeably now.

He could see the Kavanaugh doll's reflection as well. It was still smirking under its cap, its cheeks the same merry pink.

As if she had suddenly seen what her father had just seen, the young girl took a step back from the window, the light in her blue eyes extinguished, her smile now overtaken by a vague sense of alarm.

"She knows," said the voice.

Cavanaugh felt his feet slowly begin to back away beneath him, as he watched the young child through the window, her freckled face barely visible through the glass now, an apparition receding into the dark background of the house.

"Time to flee," said the voice.

Cavanaugh turned around and looked at the house across the street. Another shade was now open in one of the other windows—this one on the ground floor of the house—the borders of its frame filled in with yet another shadow.

Or was it the same shadow in a different room of the house?

Cavanaugh walked briskly away from his front yard, his daughter's doll in one hand, his briefcase full of nothing in the other. As he made his way down the road, he broke into a slow trot, houses on either side of his path.

Shades opened.

Shadows appeared.

They were all watching him.

Sweat trickled down from his brow and sideburn.

His pants were heavy and wet.

Somewhere down the road, a dog barked.

CAVANAUGH MISSES THE BUS

THE YOUNG BOY walked into the kitchen the next morning and saw his mother gazing out the window at nothing in particular, her barrette and bra strap back in their upright positions.

"Mom? Mom?" said the boy. "Who was he, Mom? Who was he?"

"Oh, I think you know who already," said the boy's mother. "I don't think I need to tell you who. You already know who, so why should I have to tell you who?"

"Tell me, Mom," said the boy. "Tell me who he was. I want to hear you tell me who he was. I want to hear you say his name out loud."

"Oh, you silly boy," said the boy's mother. "You silly, silly boy. Can't you hear it? Can't you hear it coming? It's the bus. It's coming. Up the road. Can't you hear it? Can't you hear it coming up the road? Hurry on now or you'll miss it. Don't worry about me now. This is not a time to worry about me. It is a time to catch the bus. So, go out there and catch it. Don't just stand there. Go out and catch that bus."

"But, Mom—" said the boy.

"Don't worry about me," said the boy's mother. "You can't protect me from him anyway. You're just a boy. And you can't stay here now anyhow. You have a bus to catch. Besides, you know I can't drive you there. I'm not one for driving—you know that. Too many cars. Too many cars with too many people in them. And the bikes."

"The bikes?" said the boy.

"The bikes," said the boy's mother. "The bikes and the people who ride the bikes. There are just too many of them on the road. Just way, way too many. Just way, way too many to worry about if you ask me. But don't ask me. You'll see for yourself one day. Driving a car is one thing, but missing the bus—well, that's another. Missing the bus—well, that means missing school, and if you miss school, then what? So, hurry on now. Just hurry on. Hurry on and catch that bus."

By the time the young boy opened the front door of the house and stepped out, he could no longer hear the sound of the big, yellow bus chugging up the road, but he ran to the bus stop regardless, a knapsack full of textbooks and binders jingling against his back as he ran. When he reached the bus stop, he found it vacant, save for a lone bench. Removing his knapsack from his back, the boy sat on the bench and listened for any sound that might give him comfort.

A cicada rattling.

A sparrow chattering.

A lone dog barking down the road.

Cavanaugh Lets the Phone Ring (and Ring)

CAVANAUGH FOUND another bus, at another station, at another hub of the neighborhood, and got on it.

This bus had other passengers on it.

Some whispered.

Others peered out the window.

The driver blurted out the names of the stops as he steered the steering wheel.

Passengers got on the bus.

Passengers got off the bus.

The sun began to sink.

Cavanaugh began to doze. He had been asleep for only a minute or two, when he heard a ringing coming from his pocket. He took the phone out and looked at the screen.

It was O'Reilly again.

Cavanaugh stared at O'Reilly's number flashing on the screen of his phone, then gazed out the window, as the bus went up one avenue, then down another.

What in the world does he want from me? Cavanaugh wondered.

The phone rang a few more times before going to voicemail.

No message was left.

A few moments later, the phone rang again, and again O'Reilly's number came up.

"Must be important," said the voice inside his head.

"Let it ring," said Cavanaugh.

It went to voicemail again, and, again, no message was left.

Cavanaugh put the ringer on mute.

He watched his phone flash in silence as O'Reilly's number came up again and again, and, again and again, no message was left.

With the Kavanaugh doll in the crook of his arm and his briefcase full of nothing on his lap, Cavanaugh closed his eyes, and as the bus chugged up one hill and down another, he drifted into a deep and heavy sleep.

Cavanaugh Gets Back to Work

When he woke up, Cavanaugh found himself at his desk, in his cubicle, inside his office. He could not remember how or when he got there.

In front of him, on his desk, were three items: the Kavanaugh doll, his briefcase full of nothing, and a brown paper bag with an open bottle of beer inside it.

Cavanaugh was so startled by this, that he tipped backward in his swivel chair and crashed to the floor. He shot right back to his feet and stepped away from his cubicle.

He peeked into the hallway to see if anyone else was in the office, and though the lights and desktops were on everywhere, there were no signs of co-workers working late.

"Thank god it's Friday."

"Who said that?" said Cavanaugh.

"I said that," said the voice.

Cavanaugh returned to his desk inside the cubicle. As he lifted the chair off the floor, he noticed that his smartphone had fallen as well.

He picked the phone up from the floor: eight calls from O'Reilly, no voice messages.

And two text messages from Mrs. Cavanaugh.

The first text message from Mrs. Cavanaugh: *When are you coming home? Working late again? I think our little one had a rough day today. In her room with the door closed since I've come home. Won't talk. Maybe she misses her dad. Come home ASAP.*

Then, nearly an hour later, the second text message from Mrs. Cavanaugh: *We need to talk.* Underneath the text was a short video. Cavanaugh pressed the play button and watched as a squirrel pranced on the Cavanaugh front lawn, a barf-stained undershirt dangling from its mouth.

How was the meat lasagna, Cavanaugh?

It had only been one night since he had heaved out his wife's meat lasagna, but it seemed like ages ago to Cavanaugh.

He replayed the video a few times, his phone still on mute, then a few more times with the volume turned up so that he could hear the sounds of it.

Cavanaugh had heard the sounds before: it was the kind of sounds that a neighborhood makes when no one is looking.

A cicada rattling.

A sparrow chattering.

A garage door opening.

A car door closing.

A tree rustling.

A train whistling.

A lone dog barking down the road.

CAVANAUGH GOES INTO HIDING

A KEYCHAIN jingling—Cavanaugh knew that sound as well.

Belt against buckle.

Boot against wood.

From under his desk, that sound had awoken Cavanaugh—the jingling sound. It was coming from outside his office room.

How long had he been napping there, all curled up under his desk, Cavanaugh had not a clue. The line between consciousness and unconsciousness had become blurry to him.

Inside his office room, the clap-on lights were now off. Had he clapped them off, or was there some central control in the building that turned all the lights out at a certain time?

He was about to get out from under his desk, when, suddenly, the lights in his office came on.

The jingling sound was louder now—it was coming from the other side of the wall of the cubicle inside his office.

Belt against buckle.

Boot against wood.

Cavanaugh had just poked his head out from under his desk, when he heard the sound of a vacuum cleaner roaring to life, all but drowning out the jingling sound.

He quickly drew himself back under the desk and pulled his knees to his chest. Still, Cavanaugh could see a pair of work boots moving from where he sat and could hear the banging of the head of the vacuum cleaner against the base of the wall, the wall of the desk, the wheel of the swivel chair.

It was as if the vacuum cleaner was searching for him, coaxing him to come out from hiding.

Hiding? Hiding from what? Cavanaugh was not sure from what, but hiding he was.

The roar of the vacuum came to a sudden halt and the jingling sound started up again. Something was being lifted off then placed back on his desk above him. When he heard the repetitive snapping sound, he knew it could only be one thing: the bobblehead doll.

As the bobblehead doll snapped on and off, laughter filled the room. He thought the laughter was coming from the doll at first—perhaps a special mechanical feature he had overlooked—but then quickly realized it was the laughter of whomever was pressing down on the doll's button above him. The laughter was of the hysterical kind, one full of snorts and wheezes aplenty.

"And jingling," said the voice.

Each time the snapping stopped, the button would be pressed, and the snapping and laughter would begin anew. As the snapping continued, the laughter went up one octave, then another octave, then another. Cavanaugh could hear the sound of a hand slapping down on the top of the desk as the man laughed—and with a slap and a laugh such as this, Cavanaugh knew that the one doing this slapping and laughing had to be a man despite not being able to see the slapping laugher's face. And Cavanaugh did not have to see the slapping laugher's face to know there were tears in his laughter, the frenetic movements of the doll having somehow broken and released some hidden dam from within.

As the slapping laugher slapped his hand against the desktop to the snapping rhythm of the doll, the clap-on bulbs from the ceiling above turned on then off, off then on, transforming Cavanaugh's cubicle into a frenzied disco of sound and light.

For a moment, the riotous laughter reminded Cavanaugh of his daughter, her head bobbling about in imitation of the bobblehead, his wife reacting in kind. Only this man that was in the room with him was different: this man could not stop. The laughter was uncontrollable.

There was another pounding of hand against desktop.

Then another.

And another.

On then off, off then on went the clap-on lights.

And then, suddenly, something shattered and the room went black.

After a brief moment of silence, the slapping laugher clapped his hands, and the clap-on lights went from off to on again.

Cavanaugh heard another jingling sound, this one more truncated. It was the sound of a keychain full of keys—he did not have to see it to know it.

"Ah, shit," said a voice.

Cavanaugh covered his mouth. *Was that my own voice that said that? Or was that the voice inside my head?*

"No," whispered the voice inside his head. "That voice is the voice of the janitor."

Cavanaugh nodded and whispered back: "The janitor."

The jingling grew louder. Cavanaugh could see the keys but not the face of the janitor, as the janitor knelt on one knee and picked up the shards of glass scattered about the wet carpet. There were several keys, each a different shape and size, all attached to a large key ring that was hooked to the janitor's brown belt.

From under his desk, Cavanaugh could smell the spilt beer on the carpet and the smoky odor of the janitor's hands. Together, it made the room smell like a bar to him.

Cavanaugh licked his parched lips.

"I could use a drink," said the voice.

With the headless janitor now only inches from his face, Cavanaugh read the name above the chest pocket on the buttoned shirt of his uniform.

"Brett," he whispered.

"Who said that?" barked the janitor.

The hands of the janitor, which had been prying bits of glass from the carpet, came to a sudden stop, and all Cavanaugh could now hear was the sound of the janitor's heavy breathing. The two men waited for some kind of sign, some kind of movement, but neither budged.

"Any one in here?" bellowed the janitor.

Cavanaugh looked at the name on the shirt again, thinking perhaps he had seen it wrong, but still, there it was: Brett.

Minutes later, the name rose out of sight, and the sound of heavy breathing came to an end, as the janitor, having pried the remaining bits of glass from the carpet, finally hoisted himself up from the floor.

With another round of clapping, the lights in the office turned off again. Even after the vacuum cleaner was pushed out of view, Cavanaugh remained under his desk regardless, his head bouncing about in the dark, listening to the jingling sound of the janitor's keys as they echoed down the hallway beyond.

Somewhere among the outer cubicles, a phone rang.

Cavanaugh's Daughter Loves Grapes

She finally decided to look it up.

Her dictionary—the one her father had given her a few months prior but had gone unopened—was sitting on its side at one end of the top shelf above her desk.

She hoisted herself up onto the desk and reached her arm as high up as she could reach it. Her fingertips were able to graze the dictionary just enough that she was able to nudge it off the edge of the shelf.

The big, black book of words hit her shoulder on the way down, banged off the edge of the desk, then hit the floor with a tremendous thud.

Her mother called up from downstairs. "Is everything alright up there, angel?"

Cavanaugh's daughter rubbed her shoulder. She could feel the mild bruise taking shape under her shirt.

"Yeah, Mommy. Everything's fine."

She quietly got down from the desk, then shut her bedroom door. She then opened her desk drawer and pulled out the folded sheet of loose-leaf paper. She unfolded it and read it again.

Brett Kavanaugh is a rapist.

She sat on the floor and opened the dictionary to the first page. It had the type of smell to it that things new or untouched had that reminded her of her mother's nail polish.

She remembered her father saying to her that you could look up any word in the dictionary and find out its meaning, and that every word was listed in alphabetical order.

She placed her tiny index finger on the sheet of paper directly on the only word she did not understand: *rapist.*

She began to flip the pages forward and at random.

c.

g.

k.

n.

q.

s.

s? She knew she had gone too far.

She flipped back.

ri-.

re-.

More *re-.*

ra-.

She skimmed down the page.

rabbit.

rabble.

rabble-rouser.

rabid.

rabies.

She flipped forward.

race.

rack.

radar.

radical.

radius.

She knew she was getting closer.

raft.

rag.

rake.

rally.

ramification.

Her finger moved faster.

rant.

rap.

Rapa.

rapacious.

rape.

rapid.

rapid-fire.

rapidity.

And then: *rapist.*

She had found it—finally. There it was, all in lowercase for her to read.

A chill went up her spine. She was not certain what it was she was so afraid of.

She looked at the word again: rapist *n.* one who rapes. *pl.* rapists.

She did not know what the *n.* or *pl.* meant, but she could read and understand the next two words: *one who . . . rapes?*

What was *rapes?* she wondered. Looks like *grapes* without the *g*, so they probably sound the same way, she figured.

Cavanaugh's daughter loved grapes—the purple kind, especially. It was the only type of fruit that she could ever stomach.

She skimmed back up the page.

rapidity.

rapid-fire.

rapid.

rape.

She followed the words that came after *rape* with her finger still on the page. They were words that she had, for the most part, never seen before: *unlawful sexual activity and usually sexual intercourse carried out forcibly or under threat of injury against a person's will.* Then down lower: *to commit rape on.* DESPOIL.

DESPOIL?

She could barely sound out a single word, let alone understand one—including, still, the very word to which the definition was assigned: *rape.*

And without her understanding of the word *rape*, she knew there would be no understanding of the word that was the original subject of her inquiry: *rapist.*

She closed the book. She imagined calling for her father. *If Daddy were here, I'd go and ask him what rape and rapist meant.*

But he was not there.

Oh, how she already missed him. If her mother was right about it, it could be several days before she would see him again.

Holding his briefcase in one hand.

Holding her bobblehead in the other.

Maybe I could just ask Mommy, she thought, but quickly cast that thought aside. What if *rapist* was a word that she was not supposed to know or say out loud? After all, who would ever trust those Tomboy—

"Honey, dinner's ready," called her mother from downstairs. "Come on down."

Cavanaugh's daughter slid the dictionary under her bed and ran out of her bedroom, toward the top of the staircase.

"Coming, Mommy."

She skipped down the stairs and into the kitchen. When she entered the room, her mother turned around from the oven with a plateful of something brown-looking.

"What's *that*?"

"Meatloaf," her mother said.

"I thought we were going to have leftover meat lasagna from the other night."

"Your father finished it all."

"When's he coming back?"

"I told you. Soon."

"How soon?"

"Eat your dinner."

"I'm not hungry."

"Eat it anyway."

Cavanaugh's daughter ate her dinner at a rapid pace until there was nothing left on her plate, despite her misgivings about the meal's appearance. After she helped put the plates away in the dishwasher, the young girl turned to her mother.

"Hey, uh, Mommy?" she said.

"Yes, angel?"

"What's a dyke?"

Cavanaugh Begins to Simmer and Swell

From somewhere in his cubicle, the phone rang, awaking him once again, for waking up to the ringing of a phone had become a new habit for Cavanaugh. When he opened his eyes, he found himself still on the floor under his desk—this time curled up against the Kavanaugh doll.

He was uncertain how the Kavanaugh doll had been placed there, and that uncertainty unnerved him some.

He slipped his hand into his pants pocket and took out his phone, but seeing that the phone was no longer charged, he quickly realized that the phone that was ringing was the one on top of his desk.

Aside from his daughter's teacher, no one had called Cavanaugh at his desk for days.

He tried to get out from under his desk but ended up banging his head against it. By the time he got his hand on his desk phone, the ringing had already stopped, and the call had been forwarded to voicemail.

Cavanaugh picked up the entire phone unit, sat down, and placed it on his lap. After the blinking red light on the unit stopped its blinking, he placed the handset to his ear and pressed the play button to listen.

It was Mrs. Cavanaugh.

"Cavanaugh? Where the heck are you? I've been trying to reach you on your cell, but you haven't responded. It's Saturday morning. Are you even alive? Look, I know what happened—between the way our poor, little angel said you looked and all that barfed-up lasagna on your undershirt, I get the picture, believe me. But it's alright, Cavanaugh. People make mistakes. People relapse—even fathers. Just come home, okay? Or at least call so we can talk. By the way, O'Reilly came by. He said he stopped by your office yesterday morning, and said there was no sign of you there. He seemed very excited to tell you something, but he didn't want to leave a message with me. He said he needed to tell you whatever he needed to tell you in person.

He asked how I was doing and asked how our little one was doing, and told me how his own little one loved our little one so much, and so I told him how our little one was feeling down and not coming out of her room, that she missed both you and that bobblehead doll you gave her. But then, without missing a beat, he said, 'I know just the thing to cheer her up.' And so he left the house for a bit—I wasn't really sure at first if he was ever going to come back at all—but then he came back about twenty minutes later, holding a plastic handbag. He asked if our little one was still upstairs in her room, and I said she was, so he went upstairs. I tried to keep up with him, but he was skipping steps on the way up, and by the time I caught up with him, he was already knocking on her bedroom door. He said, 'Little angel, little angel'—that's what he said, I swear it—he said, 'Little angel, little angel, it's Uncle O'Reilly—may I come in and give you something?' And you know what our little angel did? She opened the door right then and there—she really did, Cavanaugh!—she opened the door right then and there with a big smile on her little face, and that O'Reilly, he came right into her bedroom and went right on over to where her nightstand was, reached into that plastic handbag he was holding, and pulled out a doll—the same bobblehead doll you had gotten at her at the ballgame!—and placed it right there on her nightstand. Said it was his daughter's, but said she could have it. Well, that little angel of ours—she couldn't believe her eyes. She was so excited, she started jumping up and down, up and down, but then O'Reilly—he said, 'Wait, wait,' and then he raised his finger up in the air—he looked possessed for a moment, O'Reilly did—and then his finger, it came swooping right down onto the doll's button—you know, the button to make its head bobble?—and bobble it did, and before you knew it, there was O'Reilly, bobbling his own head—up and down, up and down—right along with it. Our little angel—she laughed so hard watching O'Reilly bobbling his head off that it got me laughing as well. That O'Reilly—he just kept just bobbling and bobbling and bobbling that big head of his, and then the three of us, we just—"

Cavanaugh heard the message cut out—it had run over the time limit—and stared into the dark of his cubicle.

O'Reilly.

The name simmered and burned in his brain.

O'Reilly.

A man whom he had seen only two nights earlier whimpering alone on his couch.

O'Reilly.

A man on the verge of losing his wife and daughter.

O'Reilly.

Hey, man, haven't you ever done something like that to a girl, or, I mean, a woman before?

O'Reilly.

You know, like, not like rape maybe, but maybe gone a little further than you should've?

O'Reilly.

. . . he came right into her bedroom and went right on over to where her nightstand was . . .

O'Reilly.

In Cavanaugh's house, in Cavanaugh's daughter's bedroom, with Cavanaugh's daughter and Cavanaugh's wife.

O'Reilly.

The three of them, together. The three of them, together, bobbling their heads to the Brett Kavanaugh bobblehead doll.

O'Reilly.

Like one little, happy family.

O'Reilly.

Cavanaugh slammed the handset down on his lap but missed the cradle. He could feel his scrotum immediately begin to swell.

"I could use a drink," said the voice.

Cavanaugh sank from his chair onto the floor, and whimpered into the dark.

Mrs. Cavanaugh Drives to the Office

SHE BEGAN to worry. It had already been a few days since she had last seen or heard from her husband. She had not witnessed what her daughter had witnessed—Cavanaugh, holding his briefcase in one hand, the bobblehead doll in the other, his head twitching about, his face scruffy and pale, peering through the window, then moving away from it—but she got the picture and knew what it all meant: her husband was off the wagon.

Off the wagon and on the bus.

Up the hill, then down the hill.

Here, then not here.

That was Cavanaugh.

She looked out her kitchen window, half-expecting to see the same face her daughter had seen just days earlier.

Maybe he's at work, she thought. After all, he did say he was in the office in those first couple of texts. Perhaps there were some half-truths mixed in with the lies.

The lies—that was what angered Mrs. Cavanaugh the most. She knew it was just the alcohol talking, but it infuriated her just the same.

She figured that even if he was not in the office at this moment, perhaps one of his co-workers could offer some more information.

She turned her gaze from the window and grabbed her car keys. She was already behind schedule for the day just thinking about Cavanaugh—and that was the name she always saw in her head whenever she thought of him now: Cavanaugh—but she decided she would stop by his office first before heading over to her own.

As she pulled her station wagon out of the garage, down the driveway, and onto the street, she heard a dog bark behind her.

She stopped the station wagon short and looked over her shoulder, but saw nothing there.

She continued down the street. As she passed by the O'Reilly house, she thought about stopping by there to see if O'Reilly had, by some chance, been in communication with her husband, but as she passed, she saw Mrs. O'Reilly, still in her night robe, tossing a full bag of trash into the garbage bin at the foot of the O'Reilly driveway.

Mrs. Cavanaugh nodded her head at Mrs. O'Reilly as she passed, but Mrs. O'Reilly did not nod her head in return.

Perhaps she did not see me, figured Mrs. Cavanaugh. Or maybe that is what a wife of an alcoholic does when a neighbor passing by in a blue station wagon nods hello: she ignores it.

Mrs. O'Reilly looked tired and irked to Mrs. Cavanaugh, but who could blame her?

Mrs. Cavanaugh turned on the radio. Maybe someone on the airwaves would say something about her husband's whereabouts.

She tuned into one station, then flipped to another, and then another.

She then switched from AM to FM. Perhaps he'll be one of those twenty-fifth callers calling into the station for concert tickets. She and Cavanaugh—they had not been to a concert in years, not since their daughter was born.

But she already knew: he was probably too drunk to call into a station or know of any concerts coming to town—or to even count to twenty-five.

She drove the station wagon uphill, then downhill, then back up the hill again. Within minutes, she had reached her husband's office plaza, the all-glass building reflecting the light-gray color of the sky above.

Her husband had been working in the very same building, in the very same company, in the very same position for years now.

He was a pencil-pusher.

A number-cruncher.

A middling, middle-aged middleman, now drunk and on the loose.

She parked her station wagon in the lot and walked across the plaza, toward the front entrance of the glass office building.

Somewhere on her neck, she felt a raindrop.

Cavanaugh Waits for the Ding

He heard the sounds of his fellow number-crunchers arriving at their cubicles: the ding of the elevator doors opening, the din of light conversation, the shuffle of feet on tile and on carpet, the opening and closing of desk drawers, the booting up of computers, the zim-zam of electronics zapping to life.

Someone, a man, asked someone else how her weekend was.

Weekend? Cavanaugh could not believe his ears. Was it Monday already?

He crawled out from under his desk. He went to check his smartphone for the time of day, but then remembered that it was still uncharged. He had not planned to not come home when he had hopped on the bus to work on Friday morning, and thus had not taken his charger with him.

Cavanaugh needed someone else's charger to recharge, but Cavanaugh was loath to ask someone and to make his presence known, given the condition he knew he was in. Other than the encounter with his daughter through the window, he had not really seen himself in the mirror in a few days, let alone bathed.

Since Cavanaugh wanted to keep his job, he came up with a plan: he would steal someone's charger. Everyone in the firm had the same model smartphone—the company had issued one to each of them—so anyone's charger would do. All he had to do was sit and wait for the sounds of someone getting up from his or her desk chair, and then pounce. Cavanaugh was a master at detecting such sounds—co-workers sipping coffee, picking up their phones, hanging up their phones, stretching their arms, cracking their knuckles—even when such sounds originated from a good distance.

He poked his head out from his cubicle. Of course, no one noticed. When it came to Cavanaugh, no one ever noticed.

The first sound of a chair being pushed aside was a false alarm: it was the guy who liked putting his clients on speaker phone so everyone could hear that he had clients to speak to. This was the same guy who also liked to tap his knuckles on his desk while he spoke. Cavanaugh had never seen his face before but knew his voice well. It was the voice of a senior-executive-in-the-making, a voice of a man going places in this world, but, unfortunately for Cavanaugh, the men's restroom was not one of those places at the moment.

"I'll send you the estimates for the quarter," said the knuckle-tapper with a tap of his knuckles. "Think you're going to be more than a little happy with them."

Cavanaugh waited for another anonymous voice in the office to give him hope. It took several minutes to come, but came it did.

"Alright, I'll meet you in the lobby in two minutes."

It was the voice of a female. A young associate perhaps. Or maybe an intern.

Cavanaugh heard the clack of phone against phone cradle, the squeak of chair wheels against carpet, the zip of a coat zipper zipping up, the click of high-heels against tile, then a mechanical ding, followed by the automated whir of elevator doors opening and shutting.

Cavanaugh knew that her workstation had to be far down the office wing, but he figured it would be his best hope. With the Kavanaugh doll in one hand and his briefcase full of nothing in the other, he got down low to the floor, though it was likely unwarranted—the cubicle walls ran high everywhere—and scurried down the wing, not stopping until he reached an alcove across from an empty workstation. He looked both ways, ducked, then scooted into the cubicle of the workstation.

There were papers and post-its everywhere. Photos tacked on the wall—family, friends, a boyfriend perhaps. A half-finished pack of breath mints. An unopened bottle of spring water. A scent of perfume—one of those cheaper brands, most likely.

It took a while for Cavanaugh to spot it, but there it was, the young woman's charger, plugged into an outlet under her desk, detached from the cell phone at the other end. Its color was a neon rainbow.

Cavanaugh was surprised the company had even made such an edition available.

He grabbed the charger, shoved it in his pocket, then poked his head out again.

No sign of the young woman.

No sign of anyone else either.

He slipped out of the cubicle, and headed for the elevator.

Still, no one.

He could hear the ding of the elevator even before he made it there. He ran and hopped on.

Not bad for someone who has not consumed anything but beer in the past few days, thought Cavanaugh.

When he reached the lobby, the scent of cheap perfume came back. He could see its probable owner's small frame from behind—an intern, definitely—as she stood waiting at the reception desk for whomever needed waiting on, and standing next to her, also with her back to Cavanaugh, was another woman. This other woman was much older than the intern, her graying blonde hair pulled back in a bun, her trim, athletic figure clothed in a suit jacket and matching pants, as she leaned over the desk, chatting with the gatekeeper of the building.

"I haven't seen my husband in days," said the woman. "Has anyone seen him come in?"

It was Mrs. Cavanaugh.

Cavanaugh covered his face with his coat and bolted out the revolving front door. He darted across the plaza without breaking stride until he reached the bus station. The bus was already waiting for him— for him alone, it sometimes seemed to him—for Cavanaugh was a man whose luck with buses was greater than his luck with anything else.

He climbed aboard, and was relieved to see no one was on it, save for the bus driver.

No one would recognize him anyway, he figured—not in the condition he was presently in. Not even his wife.

"Missus Cavanaugh," whispered the voice inside his head.

There she was, exiting the building and holding her coat against her chest, as the wind blew across the plaza and the raindrops became heavier.

Cavanaugh watched her through the window of the bus, as she made her way over to the parking lot where her station wagon—*their* station wagon—was more-than-likely parked.

She did not look concerned to Cavanaugh.

Not worried.

Not angry.

Not sad.

She seemed, to some degree, at peace with herself.

"She wanted to make sure you were really gone before doing anything," said the voice.

Doing what? wondered Cavanaugh. A chill went up his back. He could not put his finger on it.

"I could use a drink."

"Who said that?" said Cavanaugh.

"You said that," said the voice.

"Indeed," said Cavanaugh. "Indeed."

The engine started up, and the bus began its route.

Cavanaugh looked at the empty seats around him.

"Alone again," said the voice.

"Alone at last," sneered Cavanaugh. He tapped his knuckles against his briefcase full of nothing. He looked out the window again one last time for Mrs. Cavanaugh, but Mrs. Cavanaugh was already gone.

As the bus rumbled uphill, then downhill, then back up the hill again, Cavanaugh leaned his face against the glass of the window, his head tapping against its own reflection.

"My wife," whispered Cavanaugh. "My little girl."

CAVANAUGH RECHARGES

WHEN CAVANAUGH GOT OFF the bus, he reached into his pocket, pulled out the stolen charger, and held it under his nose.

"Still smells like that perfume," said Cavanaugh aloud to himself. Cavanaugh was now saying a whole *lot* of things aloud to himself. With a charger that smelled of cheap perfume, a doll that resembled Brett Kavanaugh, and a briefcase full of nothing, Cavanaugh was going places in this world.

"But to which places?" said Cavanaugh.

"To a bar," said the voice.

"But where's the bar around here?"

Cavanaugh walked almost a half-mile downtown before finding a bar with a restaurant.

By then, he had already passed a clocktower and knew it was just past noon. The more he walked, the more he saw people emerging out onto the sidewalks from their buildings and shops and places of work for their lunch break.

Lunch.

Cavanaugh thought about that word, *lunch*, and pondered how he could have gone this long without eating. He had drunk a lot of beer over the past few days, but still, the idea that he was only beginning to feel hungry now surprised him.

He felt around his gut with his hand to see if he had lost weight, but the man-pouch was still there. He moved his hand to his face: the pockmarks were still there, too.

The neon-blue sign above the entrance read WRONG WAY COR-RIGAN'S, yet Cavanaugh was not one to divine messages from such signs, and thus entered regardless. Once inside the establishment, he did not wait to be seated, but instead, with his Kavanaugh doll in one hand and his briefcase full of nothing in the other, he sat himself down in the booth in the corner of the room.

The menus were already stacked up and folded against the wall of the booth. He took one out, opened it, and ran his finger up and down until it landed on what he was looking for.

Buffalo wings, a bucket of forty for forty dollars. With bleu cheese, an additional two dollars.

"Found what you're looking for?"

Cavanaugh looked up from the menu and saw a waitress, her pen and pad in hand. Her top was plaid and shoulderless, her pants were denim, and her mouth was chewing on something that seemed larger than chewing gum. Her hair was a light brown, and she looked tired and middle-aged to Cavanaugh, like he was, bearing no signs in her face of any makeup. Though she was a physical reflection of himself in some ways, Cavanaugh found her attractive regardless.

"Long day, eh?" said Cavanaugh. As soon as he said this, Cavanaugh wondered if it could be mistakenly taken as an insult about her exhausted appearance. Instead, the woman smiled over her pad, almost grateful, it seemed to Cavanaugh, for a few words of civil empathy.

"Well, my day just started," said the waitress, "but I'm sure it will be." She put her hands on her hips. "You, on the other hand, look like you could use a vacation." She leaned in: "Maybe a shower, too." She burst into a brief cackle. "So, what are ya, some kind of traveling salesman?"

Cavanaugh was surprised by the blunt humor aimed at his expense. He took no offense at it, however, and perhaps rather vainly, took it to be a flirtatious gesture.

He considered her question, smiled back at her, then lied: "Yup. That's what I am. A traveling salesman."

"Yeah, I figured that," said the waitress. "We get plenty of those around here. So, what are we having?"

"The buffalo wings."

"The appetizer?"

"No, the entrée. The bucket of forty for forty bucks. With bleu cheese."

"Wow, well, someone's hungry today." She pointed to the Kavanaugh doll next to him in the booth. "Guess your little friend there packs quite a mean appetite." She cackled again. "Anything else, dear?"

"A pitcher."

"A pitcher of water?"

"No, a pitcher of beer. Guinness, if you've got it."

"Oh, we've got it." She turned to the doll. "Hey, buddy, got any ID?"

Another cackle.

She scribbled on her pad. "So, the bucket of forty with bleu cheese and a pitcher of Guinness. Anything else?"

"Yeah." He pulled out the neon-rainbow charger from his coat pocket. "Do you have something I can plug this into?"

"Oh, sure," said the waitress. "There's an outlet there right under the table, honey, if you feel around for it. Ooh, what's that—neon-rainbow? Ooh, I like it. Does it glow in the dark?"

Cavanaugh had never considered whether or not his latest plunder glowed in the dark, but the idea made him curious. He did not want to come off as if the charger was actually someone else's, so he decided to lie to the waitress again.

He nodded. "Yup. It does glow in the dark. Pretty cool, eh?"

"Very cool," said the waitress with a wink. "Okay, so, I'll put this order right in, and I'll be right out with the pitcher. Let me know if you need anything else, okay?"

"Yup."

Cavanaugh plugged the charger into the outlet, then looked about the other booths.

There was no one around. No one in the eating area. No one in the bar area either.

There was a TV on mute in close-caption up high in the opposite corner of the room. Highlights of the ballgame from the night before. Some player switched teams with another player. A free agent. Like Cavanaugh.

Most of the walls of the bar and restaurant were covered with old black-and-white framed photos of men in aviator apparel sitting in cockpits or posing next to propeller planes. There was a no-smoking sign on one wall, but the whole place still reeked of smoke regardless.

Everything around Cavanaugh appeared hazy to him. He needed that pitcher.

The pitcher came.

"Here you go," said the waitress. "Anything else I can help you with while you wait for those wings?"

"Got any trail mix?"

"We got honey-roasted nuts over at the bar—want that?"

"That'll work."

"Alright, I'll bring them right over then. Wings are on the way."

After she brought over the nuts, Cavanaugh checked his phone for messages as the phone came back online and resumed its recharge.

There were three new messages, all voice. No texts. No emails.

Cavanaugh played the first message: "Oh, hi, Mister Kavanaugh. This is Missus—*oh, Missus Cavanaugh, Missus Cavanaugh!*—again, your daughter's teacher. Listen, I want to apologize for how I spoke to you last Thursday. I was way out of line. I mean, I still think your daughter needs to avoid bringing in items that might be considered culturally, or morally for that matter, controversial or offensive, but still, I should not have left off our conversation the way I had left it off. And for that, I do apologize. I mean, in case you're wondering, I sincerely am of the view that Brett Kavanaugh is a morally-corrupt, rapist low-life—not withstanding how you might, or might not, feel about him—and, you know, some of us—not necessarily me, but maybe me—have been affected personally by such issues, but that's a discussion that probably, I know, belongs outside the realm of the dynamic between teacher and parent. But at the same time, I do want to protect your daughter, for she is still very young and innocent, and I would hate to see her, even if it's unknowingly, embrace such a doll and the values it brings with it. By the way, separate from that, I just want to put out there that your daughter seemed, well, a little distraught this morning when she came to class. Not sure if it had anything to do with the Brett Kavanaugh bobblehead, or if it was something else, but I was wondering if you or Missus Cavanaugh—*But it's alright, Cavanaugh. People make mistakes. People relapse—even fathers*—were aware of anything amiss either at home or with anything else. If either you or Missus Cavanaugh can call me back so we can discuss, that would be great. My direct number here is—"

Cavanaugh clicked off the message. He could not listen any further. It pained him to feel that his decision, or indecision, had triggered such emotional trauma and anguish for another person. He had known better than to let his daughter bring that doll to school, let alone having purchased it for her in the first place. A part of him wanted to call back, or at least leave a message and let her teacher know that he, too, was no fan of Brett Kavanaugh—the real-life one, at least—but he sensed the potential danger in engaging, and was aware enough of the mental state he was currently in to know that now was not the best time to express his feelings on the subject, or on anything in regard to his daughter or Kavanaugh.

Kavanaugh. The name alone made Cavanaugh sick to his stomach, but not sick to the point of not being able to enjoy the pitcher of Guinness that was presently in front of him, or the giant bucket of buffalo wings that was, at that very moment, en route to his table.

"Here's your bucket, hon'," said the waitress. "And here is your bleu cheese. Enjoy!"

Cavanaugh was about to play the second and third messages on his phone but decided to let it wait. No reason to spoil the mood or his meal any further. No, this was a time for Cavanaugh himself to recharge, no matter how short-lived that time might be.

He pulled the first wing from the bucket, dipped it in bleu cheese, and opened his mouth.

CAVANAUGH GETS A WAKE-UP CALL

Wake up!

Wake up right now or you're gonna miss the bus!

Wake up and catch that bus!

Hurry up and catch it before it's too late!

You can't protect me, you silly boy—it's too late!

It's too late, you silly, silly, silly boy!

Lord knows I can't drive you there!

Too many cars!

Too many bikes!

Too many roads!

Too many signs!

Too many people!

Too many everything!

So, wake up, silly boy!

Wake up right now and run after that bus before it's too late!

And don't forget your lunch box this time.

CAVANAUGH ROOMS WITH KAVANAUGH

CAVANAUGH OPENED HIS EYES and found himself on his knees with his head twitching and his face hovering over the rim of a toilet bowl whose insides and perimeter were all glutted up with his own vomit. The stench of buffalo sauce slicked in stomach acid wafted up his nose.

"Buffalo barf," said the voice. "Yum."

Cavanaugh considered his white button-down shirt for a moment: no barf there. Not such bad aim for a man who blacked out.

He was able to recall a bit of what happened earlier that day, after he had left the restaurant, but not much. He had gotten on a bus again—that much he remembered. And at one of the stops, he had found the word he was looking for—it was on a sign, all lit up in neon: MOTEL.

"I'm at a motel," said Cavanaugh.

"You are at a motel," confirmed the voice.

"This is my barf," said Cavanaugh.

"That is your barf," confirmed the voice.

He remembered the waitress, the pale, freckled skin of her bare shoulders, her cackle. He tried to recall where they had left off.

How was that bucket, Mister Cavanaugh? Is there anything else I can get you?

Another pitcher would be great.

Are you sure, Mister Cavanaugh? You've already had three.

More like two and a half. There was a lot of ice in that last one.

You're not going to be driving on the road today, are ya, Mister Cavanaugh?

Nope. Missus Cavanaugh—she does most of the driving, not me. I'm more of a bus person. Say, how do you know my name is Cavanaugh?

You've been in conversation with yourself at this booth for the past two hours—that's how.

Oh, I see—eavesdropping now, are we?

Yeah, yeah. I'll bring ya another half-pitcher, Mister Cavanaugh. Then you'll have to go.

Go? Go where?

Home. To Missus Cavanaugh. I'm sure she misses you.

Mrs. Cavanaugh.

Cavanaugh rose unsteadily from the bathroom floor, his head reeling.

Mrs. Cavanaugh.

Cavanaugh recalled nothing after that half of a pitcher. Only fragments.

MOTEL—he remembered that.

Was it the Sunrise or the Sunset Motel? He could not recall which.

Better poke my head out and have a look, he figured. Perhaps things will come back to me then.

Cavanaugh lumbered halfway across the bedroom—it was too dim to see much—and was about to draw the window shades, when he spotted the minibar below the TV stand.

"You could use a drink," said the voice.

"No, I fucking couldn't," said Cavanaugh, his voice echoing off the walls of the room.

"Oh, go on," said the voice. "Go on and have a look at least."

Cavanaugh crouched down and opened the door of the minibar. Peanuts, pretzels, chips, cheese and crackers, chocolate kisses, a couple of bottles of spring water, a few cans of German beer, a mini-carton of fruit juice, and, stuffed all the way in the back behind an aging apple, about a half-dozen small bottles of the hard stuff.

Cavanaugh reached all the way in and took one of the bottles of hard stuff out, and inspected it.

MADE IN IRELAND.

"Ah, the homeland," said Cavanaugh.

"See that?" said the voice. "I told you it was worth the look."

Cavanaugh looked around the room. No one was watching. Just a small room with a twin bed. The neon-rainbow charger and his briefcase full of nothing were on the floor near the doorway. There was a small, round eating table with two chairs in the corner of the room by the door. On the center of the table stood the Kavanaugh doll. It was staring right at him, smirking.

For a moment, Cavanaugh thought about the replacement Kavanaugh doll that O'Reilly had given to his daughter, its head bobbling about, standing watch as she slept, before his thoughts then turned to O'Reilly being in her bedroom as well with his own head bobbling about.

Cavanaugh held the tiny bottle of hard stuff to his chest and took a big whiff of the room.

The smell of barf was everywhere. Had he not made it to the toilet in time? He looked about his feet, and proceeded carefully to the bed, tiptoeing around any potential unseen chunder that might crunch under his feet. When he reached the bed, he laid himself down and propped himself up against one of the pillows.

He was in the midst of guzzling the tiny bottle down, when he heard a jingling sound.

Cavanaugh rose from the pillow. What was that? he wondered. And where was it coming from?

Looking around from his perch on the bed, he caught a glimpse of his reflection on the empty TV screen above the dresser. He grabbed the remote from the nightstand next to the bed—*right on that nightstand, watching over her*—and powered up the cable.

Cavanaugh finished off the rest of the bottle, got up from the bed, opened the minibar door again, seized all the remaining tiny bottles of hard stuff, and went back onto the bed.

Something wet did crunch under his sock this time, but he paid it no mind.

He twisted open one of the bottles and looked up at the screen.

More ballgames, more highlights. And one more trade. A man for another man. A bartering of restricted free agents.

How can one be both restricted and free at the same time? wondered Cavanaugh.

He took another gulp, and then watched as the TV switched to a men's shaving cream commercial. A man—a retired football jock whom Cavanaugh had not seen in years—lathered up his face before shaving his facial stubble with a disposable razor.

"A perfect shave," said the retired football jock.

"A perfect slider," said the voice.

Cavanaugh placed his hand to his cheek and stroked its roughness, then smelled underneath his arm. He now wondered if it was he or the room that smelled like vomit.

Another jingling sound.

Jingle-jingle.

Jingle-jingle.

Cavanaugh placed the tiny bottle on the nightstand and listened. It was coming from somewhere beyond the confines of the room.

Perhaps from outside, Cavanaugh figured.

He picked up a new bottle, twisted the cap off, and resumed his binge.

Cavanaugh returned his gaze to the screen. Another ceremonial first pitch from another political figure. This time, a mayor.

Will you all please rise and give a warm hero's welcome . . . Ladies and gentlemen, here he is, defender of our Constitution . . . Justice . . . Brett . . . Kavanaugh.

Cavanaugh could still see Kavanaugh's slow yet confident trot to the mound in his head.

The waving of the cap.

The shit-eating grin.

We love you, Brett!

Cavanaugh took another swig and glanced over at the table, the Kavanaugh doll still staring right at him.

Of course it's still staring right at me, thought Cavanaugh. It couldn't be looking anywhere else unless I had moved it, could it?

Cavanaugh looked back at the TV.

"Brett."

"Who said that?" Cavanaugh pulled the bottle from his lips and listened.

"Oh, Brett."

Was that the voice inside his head? Or was someone eavesdropping on his thoughts? Which was it?

"Oh, god, Brett."

Cavanaugh shot up from his bed. How could it be? How could someone have heard what he was thinking?

"Yes, Brett."

"Oh, yes, Brett."

"Oh, yes, god, oh, Brett."

Another jingling sound, louder this time.

A squeaking.

Jingling and squeaking.

And then against the wall behind him—BANG!

The tiny bottle went airborne across the room from Cavanaugh's hands, as he turned to hide under the bed covers. A ghost was on the loose.

"Oh, Brett."

"Oh, yes, god, oh, Brett."

"Oh, fuck me, Brett."

Fuck me, Brett? Cavanaugh lifted his head from under the covers.

"Oh, fuck me, Brett. Fuck me harder."

More squeaking.

More jingling.

The wall vibrated.

The bed shook.

The alarm clock fell and crunched against the floor.

The Kavanaugh doll tipped about the tabletop but held its ground, still managing to keep its stare and smirk squarely aimed at Cavanaugh.

The jingling, the squeaking, the grunting, the moaning—it was all coming from next-door, not his own room, but for a reason he could not put his finger on, this scared Cavanaugh all the more. He got up from his bed, backed away from the wall, and watched both shake in front of him.

"Brett."

"Brett."

"Brett."

"Brett."

The remaining tiny bottles of hard stuff fell to the floor. The lamp on the nightstand was about to tip over as well, but Cavanaugh caught it in the nick of time. He turned off its switch and held it there in his hands.

More squeaking.

More grunting.

More moaning.

More shaking.

More banging.

More jingling.

"Faster, Brett, faster."

"Oh, fuck me, Brett, fuck me."

"Oh, please come, Brett, please come."

More jingling.

More banging.

More snapping.

Snapping?

Cavanaugh turned toward the table. The doll had turned on by itself, its head bobbling to the rhythms being generated from the room next-door.

"Come inside me, Brett, come inside me."

"Come."

"Come."

"Come."

Jingling.

Banging.

Snapping.

Jingling.

Banging.

Snapping.

Up and down, back and forth, the head of the bobblehead went.

"Oh."

"Yes."

"God."

"Brett."

"Brett."

"Brett."

"Oh, my god."

"Brett."

Another bang and the pillow fell to the floor.

Then silence.

It was over.

O say can you see, by the dawn's early light . . .

Cavanaugh turned toward the glow of the TV screen. The ballplayers solemnly held their caps to their chests.

He faced the wall behind the bed again and listened. He could hear it just barely now, but it was still there, on the other side of the wall: a jingling sound.

Belt against buckle.

Then: the sound of footsteps.

Boot against wood.

Then, for the briefest of moments: the sound of traffic in the night.

Then another bang: a door being slammed shut.

Cavanaugh held the lamp tight to his chest and listened. He could hear the keys jingle.

"Was it him, you think?" whispered Cavanaugh to the dark and empty room. "Was it really Brett?"

"Brett?" said the voice inside his head. "You mean Brett as in Brett Kavanaugh?"

"No, not that Brett, you idiot," said Cavanaugh. "The *other* Brett. The janitor. From the office. The guy with all those keys jingling about him. Do you think it was him?"

Cavanaugh waited for a response from the voice inside his head, but none came. He was about to repeat the question aloud, when, suddenly, something from outside roared to life.

Cavanaugh could see the shadow coming through the window shade. It was a person—a man, he could tell—pushing something long and mechanical back and forth in front of himself, a thundering cane clattering against the foot of his motel room door, and, every now and then, Cavanaugh could still hear it—coming from the vague swaying about the shadow's waist—a jingle.

Cavanaugh watched the shadow in silence and waited until it disappeared from view. He then turned toward the table in the corner of the room.

The bobblehead doll stood still there in the dark, its head no longer bobbling. But its gaze was still fixed on Cavanaugh.

Cavanaugh backed away from the table, until the back of his leg bumped against the nightstand. He turned and placed the lamp back in its position, then climbed into bed, his eyes never diverting from the doll on the table, the glow of the TV making new shadows in the dark.

"Brett."

"Who said that?" said the voice.

"I said that," said Cavanaugh.

"And who are you?" said the voice.

"A pencil-pusher," said Cavanaugh. "A number-cruncher. A middling, middle-aged middleman."

Cavanaugh looked away from the table, but even with his back now turned from the window, he listened as hard as he could to the mechanical humming as it faded off down the long corridor outside his door.

Somewhere down the road from the motel, a dog barked.

THE WAITRESS DIALS NINE-ONE-ONE

Nine-one-one. How may I help you today?

"Hello. I want to report a stalker."

A stalker did you say?

"Yes, a stalker."

And who is this stalker stalking, Ma'am?

"The stalker is stalking me, sir."

Got it. And do you know the identity of your stalker, Ma'am?

"Yes. Or, I mean, I know his last name, anyway."

And what is his last name?

"His last name is Cavanaugh."

Is that Cavanaugh with a C, Ma'am, or Kavanaugh with a K?

"Um, Cavanaugh with a C, I believe."

And his first name?

"Oh, I don't know his first name."

Don't know it, eh?

"Nope. Don't know it."

So, this Cavanaugh person—is he stalking you right at this very moment, Ma'am?

"No, he is not stalking me right now, but—"

So, you're saying the stalker—this Cavanaugh fella—he is not stalking you at this very moment—is that correct?

"Yes, that is correct, but—"

So, just so we're clear on this, this is not a stalking-in-process, correct?

"No, this stalking ended about ten minutes ago."

Did you say ten minutes ago?

"Uh-huh."

And when did this stalking commence?

"Pardon?"

I said when did this stalking begin? How long did the stalking last for? Was it fifteen minutes, twenty minutes, a half-hour—

"About two minutes."

Two minutes, you say?

"Uh-huh. Two minutes."

So, this Cavanaugh fella—he stalked you for about two minutes and then just left you alone?

"Yup. Like I said, he left here about ten minutes ago. Maybe eleven or twelve by now."

And where is here?

"Sir?"

I said where is here, Ma'am. Where are you calling from?

"Oh, um, Wrong Way Corrigan's. It's a bar and—"

Yes, I know what Wrong Way Corrigan's is, Ma'am—I'm quite familiar with it. So, are you employed by Corrigan's, Ma'am?

"Uh-huh. I'm a waitress here."

And this Cavanaugh fella—is he employed there as well?

"No, he is not."

Was he ever employed there, Ma'am?

"No, he was just a customer here."

Got it. And was this the first time you were ever stalked by this Cavanaugh customer?

"Yup."

And had you ever seen him anywhere else besides Corrigan's before this incident?

"Nope."

So, what did this Cavanaugh customer do while he was there at Corrigan's? Did he shadow you around the restaurant?

"No, he sat mostly."

He sat?

"Uh-huh. He sat in the booth and ate a bucket of wings."

Wings you say?

"Uh-huh."

What kind of wings?

"The Buffalo kind."

Buffalo?

"Uh-huh. And he had a lot to drink as well."

A lot? How much is a lot?

"Like three or four orders."

You mean like three or four beers?

"No, I mean pitchers. Three or four pitchers."

Pitchers. Alright now. Got it. So, this Cavanaugh customer—would it be fair to say he was intoxicated?

"Uh-huh. I would think that's fair to say. Very fair."

Would you say very intoxicated?

"I would say very, very intoxicated."

Got it. And who was it exactly that was serving him these wings and these pitchers—was it you, Ma'am?

"It was."

And was there anyone else that was there at Corrigan's when you were serving him?

"Well, there was the kitchen staff, but they never actually saw him because they were in the kitchen cooking the whole time. And while I think the bartender showed up for the start of his shift at some point, I'm not entirely certain about that."

What about any of the other waiters or customers? Were any of them there when you were serving this Cavanaugh customer?

"Nope. It was just me. Me and Cavanaugh, I mean. Me, Cavanaugh, and that bobblehead doll of his."

Did you say bobblehead doll?

"Uh-huh. I did."

What kind of bobblehead doll?

"Um, well, it's the kind that bobbles—"

Yes, I know it bobbles, Ma'am. They all bobble. What I mean is what did the bobblehead doll look like?

"Oh, um, well, it was a bobblehead doll of one of them ballplayers— not exactly sure which one it was supposed to be though."

That's okay, Ma'am—that's good enough. Now, was there anything else in his possession at the time of this stalking?

"Anything else?"

You know, like some sort of weapon or—

"Nope, nothing like that. Just a briefcase, a phone, and a charger— those were the only other things he had with him."

"A charger, you say?"

"Uh-huh. A charger. For his phone. It was neon and colored like a rainbow. He said it glowed in the dark, but I didn't trust him."

Alright, let me write that all down . . . Neon . . . rainbow . . . charger . . . says it glowed in the dark . . . but maybe it didn't . . . Now, did he threaten you at all with his neon-rainbow charger?

"Threaten me?"

Meaning, did he ever threaten to—

"No, no, he just plugged it into the outlet underneath the table, that's all."

Got it. Now, going back to the stalking part of the incident—did that occur before, during, or after you served this Cavanaugh customer?

"It happened after. Right after."

Right after. Got it. For about two minutes you said, right?

"Yup. Two minutes."

Okay. Got it. Alrighty. Think we're done here.

"We are? But—"

Now, Ma'am, I'm going to pass this along to the investigations unit. Gonna see if they could sniff around a bit and find out more about this Cavanaugh customer. One of them will probably follow up with you in a short while and ask you some more questions.

"Well, um, that's good because there is a heck of a lot more to the story."

There always is, Ma'am. Well, alright now, you go ahead and have yourself a pleasant evening. I wouldn't worry too much about this Cavanaugh customer. We handle folks like him all the time. So don't you fret it, Ma'am.

"Alright, I'll try not to. Thanks for your help."

Sure thing, Ma'am. You take care now. So long.

"Wait—sir? Don't you need to take down my name and number? Hello? Are you still there, sir? Hello?"

CAVANAUGH ANSWERS THE DOOR

IT WAS JUST BEFORE MORNING and still dark in the motel room, when he was suddenly awoken by a jingling sound—a jingling sound that sounded different from the jingling sound he had heard just hours earlier.

It was coming from outside.

The jingling seemed to pass by his room one way at first, and then seemed to pass by it the other way before stopping right outside his door.

There was a hard knock.

Had Brett—or whoever that person who jingled about yesterday—come to clean his room?

He looked at the clock, its red digits glaring in the darkness.

He looked at the TV screen, watched the morning anchors sip away at their coffees.

It was way too early for cleaning service. Perhaps Brett had come to tell him something: that he knew it was Cavanaugh who had brought those beer bottles into his cubicle, that he knew it was he who had stolen the neon-rainbow phone charger from the intern's workstation, that it was all caught on the office security camera, and there would be no getting around it.

Or perhaps Brett just wanted to finally see what Cavanaugh looked like, to see the face of a man who hides under his own desk.

More knocking at the door—this time it was heavy and shook the room.

Cavanaugh was afraid to answer the door but was more afraid not to answer. He rolled out from the bed—he was still clad in the same business-casual office attire he had been wearing for days—and lumbered over to the door.

The knocking continued against the door even as he turned the knob and opened it.

The early morning air felt fresh against his face. He had not realized how stuffy his room had been until he had opened the door.

"Mister Cavanaugh?"

"That's me." Cavanaugh looked at the man in front of him. It was not Brett—or at least not the Brett he had imagined if the man was a Brett. What the man was though was a police officer, wearing an official blue cap and uniform, his badge level with Cavanaugh's eyes. He was taller than Cavanaugh and a bit stockier too, and though his skin was weathered and baggy around his grayish blue eyes, Cavanaugh figured the officer and he were around the same age regardless.

"Mister Cavanaugh, I'm Officer—"

"Look, I got the charger for you right here," said Cavanaugh. "It's right there on the dresser there. I was going to give it back to that intern tomorrow."

"Mister Cavanaugh?"

"I'm really sorry, Officer. It won't ever happen again, I swear."

"Mister Cavanaugh, I don't know anything about a charger, but—"

It suddenly hit Cavanaugh. "Oh, I know what this is about. It's Missus Cavanaugh—she sent you here, right? So, I guess she does miss me after all."

"No, this has nothing do with your wife—or your mother or whomever. Now, look, Mister Cavanaugh, it's—"

"Oh, my god!" Cavanaugh clasped his hands over his mouth. "Did something happen to Cavanaugh's daughter?"

"Cavanaugh's daughter?"

"Yes, Cavanaugh's daughter. Is everything all right with her? Did something happen?"

"Um, by Cavanaugh's daughter, do you mean, *your* daughter, Mister Cavanaugh?"

Cavanaugh nodded his head anxiously.

"Uh, well, no, no, Mister Cavanaugh. This has nothing to do with your daughter."

"Oh, thank goodness," said Cavanaugh, wiping his brow with the back of his hand. "Thank goodness nothing has happened to Cavanaugh's daughter."

"Look, Mister Cavanaugh. I'm not here to talk about your daughter, your wife, your mother, or anyone else. I'm here to talk about you, Mister Cavanaugh. I'm here to talk about you and what happened the other day at Corrigan's."

"Corrigan, Corrigan . . ." The name sounded vaguely familiar to Cavanaugh at first, but he struggled to put the name together with a face or an object.

"Mister Cavanaugh," said the officer, "you mean to tell me you don't remember being at Wrong Way Corrigan's the other—"

"Oh, right, right!" said Cavanaugh, as the name suddenly hit him. "Wrong Way Corrigan. That pilot who took off from Brooklyn and flew his plane to Ireland instead of California. I had read all about him on the menu they had there."

"Well, yeah," said the officer. "But I haven't come here to talk to you about Wrong Way Corrigan the pilot. What I have come here to talk to you about is Wrong Way Corrigan's, the restaurant, and what transpired there the other day."

"Right, the restaurant," said Cavanaugh. "The restaurant and bar with the TV and everything—sure, I remember it now."

"Well, I can't imagine how you wouldn't remember," said the officer. "You were there for quite some time."

"Yes—I mean, I suppose I—"

"And there was a lady there that was serving you—you remember that as well?"

"Sure, Officer. I remember her. The waitress—she brought me my bucket."

"Your bucket?"

"You know—bucket. Of wings, I mean. Buffalo wings. She brought me my pitchers, too."

"Yes, the pitchers," said the officer. "The pitchers of Guinness, right?"

"Right." Cavanaugh scratched his groin for a moment, then his head. He was not sure where this was going. "Officer, is there some—"

"She said you had more than one pitcher of Guinness—is that correct?"

"Yeah, I think I had two, or maybe—"

"You had four." The officer held the paper receipt in front of Cavanaugh's face. "See that? Four pitchers. Four pitchers in one gosh darn sitting."

"Wow." Cavanaugh scratched something inside his ear and looked at it. "Four pitchers. That sure is a whole lot of pitchers. A whole bullpen's worth, right?"

Cavanaugh chuckled awkwardly, but the officer was not amused.

"Look, Mister Cavanaugh, can we go over what occurred between you and the waitress who served you at Corrigan's?"

"Well, sure we can," said Cavanaugh. "Where would you like me to start?"

"From the beginning," said the officer.

"Alright, well, I guess the first thing she did was take my order."

"Uh-huh. What happened next?"

"She took my order and then came out with the bucket of what I ordered—the forty-for-forty special."

"The wings you mean?"

"Uh-huh."

"Buffalo wings, right?"

"Uh-huh."

"And then what happened?"

"And then she got me my pitchers."

"And then?"

"And then she said something to me."

"Said something to you?"

"Yeah, said something to me." Cavanaugh looked up at the ceiling above the doorway as he tried to jog his own memory, then looked over the police officer's shoulder at the dimly lit neon-orange sign hovering over the motel's parking lot.

SUNBURST.

Ah, that was the name. The Sunburst Motel.

"Mister Cavanaugh? Mister Cavanaugh, what was it that she said—"

"She said that I had been having a conversation with myself. Said that's how she knew my last name was Cavanaugh."

Cavanaugh looked at the officer, as he waited for his next question, but the officer seemed befuddled.

"Say," said Cavanaugh, "is that how you found out about my last name being Cavanaugh? Did you hear me talking to myself in my room here?"

"Um, no, Mister Cavanaugh. She was the one who told me—the waitress. But she also told me about that conversation you had with yourself at Corrigan's, and about how you mentioned during that conversation that you were planning on reserving a room at the nearest motel. Which is why I was able to find you here: this happens to be the nearest motel from Corrigan's, and you're checked in here under the name Cavanaugh. So, that sort of corroborated with what she told me."

"Ah," said Cavanaugh. "I see." He still had no clue what the officer wanted from him, but he wanted to end the conversation before finding out. "Well, um, look, Officer, I can understand why the waitress would be concerned about the way I was conversing with myself, or even alarmed by it, but that's—"

"But that's not why I'm here, Mister Cavanaugh."

"It's not?"

"Nope. It's not. Now, Mister Cavanaugh, I need you to recollect what happened after you paid the bill."

"*After* I paid?"

"The waitress—she tells me that you did not immediately leave your booth after you paid the bill."

"Um, I didn't?"

"Nope. Not according to her. According to her, you lingered there in your booth for several more minutes. She said that she came in and out of the kitchen multiple times, and every time she came out, you were still there, slumped in your booth with your mouth hanging open, watching her."

Watching over her.

"I was? But I don't remember any—"

"She said that she then went to the ladies' restroom, and that's where it happened."

"Where what happened, Officer? Tell me. Please tell me." Cavanaugh could not take the suspense any longer.

The officer pulled out a small pad from his back pocket and reviewed his notes. "Well, let's see here . . . According to the waitress, when she came out of the stall in the ladies' restroom, she found you there with your mouth still hanging open, waiting for her. Said you scared the living bejesus out of her, which, if you ask me, is quite understandable."

Cavanaugh shook his head. He shook his head hard, back and forth, back and forth. His head hurt when he shook it. "But it can't be, Officer. It can't—"

"She said that you then told her that she was an excellent waitress, that she was 'good at waiting'—or something like that—and that you had paid the bill in cash and had left her a thirty-percent tip, and that you didn't want to leave without saying goodbye and thank you. Said that you told her all this while holding a briefcase in one hand and a doll—a bobblehead doll, I think is what she said—in the other hand, like so."

The officer demonstrated, invisible objects in both of his large hands.

Cavanaugh could not recall any of it, but the demonstration alone was enough to convince him that he was the perpetrator. Whatever the officer had in store for him, he would have to accept and grow from it—even if it meant living behind bars for a while.

"Say," said the officer, looking past Cavanaugh's shoulder. "That doll over there on the table there—is that the bobblehead doll you brought with you to Corrigan's?"

"Well, yeah," said Cavanaugh. "I mean, maybe, I—"

"Hey, wait a minute. That doll's face—it looks familiar. Is that—is that supposed to be Brett Kavanaugh?"

Cavanaugh looked over at the doll. It was staring right at him again. Had the doll turned in the night by itself, or had he gotten up and moved it so that it would not face the bed anymore?

He prayed it was the latter.

Cavanaugh turned back toward the officer and nodded his head. "Yes, officer. It *is* him. It's Brett Kavanaugh. Or a bobblehead of him, at least."

"Oh, wow," said the officer, removing his cap, running his hand over his thick, wavy hair.

Cavanaugh could remember when *his* hair looked like that— those days before he went out into the real world, got a job, a wife, a child.

The officer put the cap back on his head. "A Brett Kavanaugh bobblehead. Very cool. Hey, that opening pitch he threw—that was something, wasn't it?"

"Yep. I was at the game."

"Yeah, I saw it on the TV. That man's sure got a mean slider, doesn't he?"

Cavanaugh nodded. He figured it would make no sense to disagree or add any nuance under the circumstances.

The officer leaned in toward Cavanaugh. "Yeah, me and my wife— we're big fans of his."

Cavanaugh gulped, as his eyes met the officer's again. "Big fans, huh? You mean of his pitching or of his judicial record?"

"Both." The officer locked eyes with Cavanaugh, took measure of him, then returned his attention to the doll. "Say, do you mind if I have a crack at that button there?"

The officer nudged his way past Cavanaugh and went over to the table. He took a whiff of the room—it still smelled like Cavanaugh's barf—wrinkled his nose with a slight grimace, then pressed the button on the base of the doll, looking on as the head bobbled and snapped away.

He smiled at Cavanaugh and nodded.

"You got yourself a really cool bobblehead there, Mister Cavanaugh," said the officer. "The folks down at the station would definitely get a kick out of this."

He pressed the button again.

"Hey, Officer," said Cavanaugh, his finger scratching behind his ear. "About that waitress—did I really actually do that thing that you said that I did? Did I really actually follow her into the ladies' restroom and scare her?"

"Well, that's what the lady said." The officer's facial expression turned solemn. "Said you pretty much—what was the word she used again?—traumatized her with the way you came at her with the doll and everything."

"*Traumatized?*" The word shook Cavanaugh to his core. Traumatizing women was something that other men did to women—men like O'Reilly, perhaps, or Brett Kavanaugh—but not he, not Cavanaugh.

It just was not possible. Or was it?

"But, Officer, I—I don't—"

"You don't recall any of that, eh?"

"No, Officer. Not at all. Really. I don't."

"Tell me something, Mister Cavanaugh: Do you recall even leaving Corrigan's?"

"Leaving?"

"Uh-huh. Leaving."

Cavanaugh thought it over hard, but no image of his departure came to mind. "Well, look, I mean, I remember entering Corrigan's, but I—"

"Don't remember leaving?"

"Yeah. I guess that part of it—leaving, I mean—that's the part I don't remember."

"How about the ladies' restroom—do you have any recollection of ever entering that room?"

"No. Not at all. Not at all, Officer. I mean, I just wouldn't do that. I just wouldn't."

"Well, she says you did do that, and that's where we have a problem."

"Look, Officer, I—"

"The good news is that you didn't touch her at all."

"No, I didn't. I mean, of course I didn't. I mean, I wouldn't, I—"

"The bad news is that she's thinking about pressing charges."

"Pressing charges?" Cavanaugh squeezed the sides of his head between his hands and shook it, back and forth, back and forth, this time even harder than when he shook it just minutes earlier. "Did you hear that? He said charges!"

The officer stepped toward Cavanaugh and leaned in. "Mister Cavanaugh? Mister Cavanaugh, who're you talking to?"

"Charges," said the voice.

"Charges," echoed Cavanaugh.

"Now, look here, Mister Cavanaugh. Why don't we just take it easy here, okay?—*Easy, Missus Cavanaugh. Easy now. Easy*—I think, from what I can see, is that this whole thing's been blown out of proportion. Maybe you were just trying to be nice, maybe you had a thing for her or something, but you were extremely drunk—drunk to the point of blackout, I'm guessing—and went about it the wrong way. For all you knew, you probably thought you had followed her into the kitchen, not the restroom."

Cavanaugh removed his hands from his head. "But, Officer, I didn't follow her, I—"

"Look, Mister Cavanaugh, we've all gone a little too far one time or another, a little further than we should've—"

"Further than we should've?" Cavanaugh thought of O'Reilly again, the phone conversation. It seemed like weeks ago, months even.

You know, like, not like rape maybe, but maybe gone a little further than you should've?

"Yep, Mister Cavanaugh," said the officer. "We've all had our moments—even us folks in blue, at times. But we're men, it happens. Right?"

"But Cavanaugh's daughter," said Cavanaugh.

"What about your daughter, Mister Cavanaugh?"

"I mean, what am I going to tell her?"

"You won't be needing to tell her anything, Mister Cavanaugh. Did you not hear what I just said? I'm going to take care of this for you. You needn't worry about a thing."

"What about the waitress?"

"What about her?"

"I mean, shouldn't I go back there and apologize to her?"

The officer grabbed Cavanaugh by the shoulders and looked him dead in the eye. "No, Mister Cavanaugh. You shouldn't. You should stay the hell away from there and let me handle it."

"But I feel terrible."

"Terrible about what?"

"About scaring her. About traumatizing her. About traumatizing that poor, nice, exhausted woman." Cavanaugh could feel the tears running down his cheeks, but the officer was having none of it.

"Look, pal. Shit happens, okay?"

"But she didn't deserve it. The waitress—she was very nice to me. Brought me my bucket, my pitchers."

"Yeah, all four of them. You know with all those pitchers she gave you, she's as much to blame as—"

"I've become an awful person. I am now an awful person."

"No, you're not, Mister Cavanaugh. You're not an awful person. You just had way too much to drink and—"

"And it's all because of that fucking doll!"

"The doll?"

"Yes, that fucking bobblehead doll right there on the table there. That fucking Brett Kavanaugh and his fucking—"

Something cold walloped Cavanaugh's cheek. It took him a moment or two to realize it had been the officer's hand that had struck flush against it.

"Never utter that man's name in vain again, you hear?" The officer was now right up in the face of Cavanaugh as the latter massaged one side of it. "Now, you listen here, you fucking whack job, and you listen up good. You need to get a goddamn hold of yourself and stay the fuck away from Corrigan's, ya hear me? Stay the fuck away and just let me take care of the situation and everything will work itself out just fine, I promise. In the meantime, take a fucking shower and clean yourself up. I could smell you all the way from my patrol car there. If there were laws against it, I'd arrest you right now just for smelling like a horse's anus."

Cavanaugh could hear the jingling sound as the officer pointed and shook his finger at him.

Must be his holster, he figured.

A sidearm perhaps.

Or perhaps handcuffs.

Some keys too, probably.

"Okay, Officer," said Cavanaugh, stroking his cheek. "I'll do what you say."

"Good." The officer took out a pen, and began to write on his pad. "Now, you mentioned a Missus Cavanaugh—is that your wife, Mister Cavanaugh?"

Cavanaugh thought for a moment. *Mrs. Cavanaugh.* She seemed so distant to him now. As if she were just a memory, an idea. But he was still very much in love with her.

"Mister Cavanaugh?"

"Yes, that's her," said Cavanaugh. "Missus Cavanaugh—she's my wife—yes."

"Would you like me to call her, Mister Cavanaugh—let her know you're okay?"

Cavanaugh looked about the officer's chest, searching for a name, but did not find one.

"Mister Cavanaugh?"

"No," said Cavanaugh. "No need to call her. I'm doing fine here. Just fine. Really. I am."

"You sure, Mister Cavanaugh?"

"I'm sure."

"Are you sure you're not in need of any medication?"

"Medication?"

"Medication for—" The officer cleared his throat. "Well, you know what for." He pointed at Cavanaugh's head. "Medication for that, I mean."

"For what?"

"For your head."

"What about my head?"

"It's shaking."

"You mean, you actually notice it shaking?"

"Well, gosh darn, Mister Cavanaugh. Of course I notice it shaking. Looks as though it's about to pop right off your neck and fly across the room."

"Oh," said Cavanaugh. "I thought I was the only one who noticed it."

The officer removed his cap and gave his head a quick scratch before returning the cap back to its position on his head. He then shoved the small pad back into the back pocket of his pants.

"Look, Mister Cavanaugh, I didn't mean you any disrespect or nothing, but all I'm saying here is you should thank your lucky stars that you have a wife that could look after you and a little girl that you could come home to."

Cavanaugh scratched his own head and nodded. "I do, Officer. I do thank my lucky stars. Every day I do. Really. I do."

"Alright, well, I'm going to go back to the station now to take care of this," said the officer. "You go get yourself cleaned up and put this behind you. And don't step foot in Corrigan's ever again, ya hear?"

Cavanaugh looked at the man's boots, his belt buckle, his badge, then spoke: "Yes, Officer. I hear you. Loud and clear."

"Good. Well, that settles it then." The officer turned from Cavanaugh and gazed past the parking lot, out toward the predawn sun beyond, its upper rim peeking out just barely over the horizon. He drew a deep breath in as if it were his last, then breathed out. "Looks like we're in for another glorious day. Luckily for me, my shift ends this morning, and I got two tickets to this afternoon's doubleheader. Going to take my son with me, speaking of children. You have a good day now, Mister Cavanaugh. Been a real pleasure."

Cavanaugh nodded and looked on as the officer jingled all the way to his patrol car. Stepping into the outer corridor of the motel, Cavanaugh watched as the car exited from the lot. He did not take his eye off the vehicle until it was down the road and out of sight.

"The coast is clear," said the voice.

Cavanaugh looked to the left of him, then to the right.

Still no sign of Brett.

He lifted his arm up and took a long, hard whiff of himself.

"Yup. A horse's anus, indeed."

Cavanaugh reentered his motel room, closed the door, and turned back toward the TV screen. He sat at the foot of his bed and gazed into the glow, his head nodding as he watched in silence.

Someone on the screen had fallen and could not get up.

Cavanaugh Heads the Wrong Way

He was on the bus again, on his way back to Wrong Way Corrigan's to apologize to the waitress, his briefcase full of nothing on his lap, the Kavanaugh doll in the seat by his side, when his phone rang.

It was O'Reilly again.

This time he was not going to ignore him. He took a deep breath and cleared his throat, not wanting to give O'Reilly any sign of the condition he was in, then answered the phone.

"Hello?"

O'Reilly was already in midstream: ". . . and I had this vision, an epiphany you can say, that if I just blocked everything out, just blocked all the bad stuff out, that I would be okay, that everything would be all right, that if I just let myself fall in love with her and let the chips fall where they would, that it would be okay. I realized that putting myself out there, and opening myself up to this sort of thing was a risk, that it made me feel vulnerable, but I knew I had to put my fear aside, I needed to show courage, or nothing will happen in my life and I'll just die, you know? And that's why I'm calling you, Cavanaugh, because I don't want to see the same thing happen to you that happened to me. No need to get ourselves stuck now. It's time to move on to the next chapter of our lives. To blaze our paths anew. Because I see the two of them almost every night now, and they've given me a second chance to make things right. Maybe it's only been a week or so, but I haven't had a drink since, and I've been to church every morning since I quit. Not saying I believe in God now or nothing, but it makes me feel good being around other people who do—the kind of people who are filled with warmth and positive energy. Positive energy—that's what this is all about, and that's what the two of them have given me. And whenever I think of the three of us together, I—"

O'Reilly's voice cut out the moment the bus went under an overpass. Cavanaugh had expected his voice to return once the bus came out the other side, but it never came back.

O'Reilly was gone for good.

Gazing out the window of the bus, Cavanaugh considered the sudden turn of events for a brief moment—O'Reilly, reunited with his family, on the road to recovery; and then there was he, Cavanaugh, in the throes of relapse, on a road, on a bus, headed downhill—but when the bus stopped at the bottom of the hill, across the street from Wrong Way Corrigan's, he quickly cast such a consideration aside.

It was time to get off the bus again.

"I could use a drink."

"Yeah, me, too," said the bus driver as Cavanaugh stepped off the bus.

Cavanaugh looked back at the bus driver, who nodded then pulled at the lever next to him to close the door shut.

Perhaps the voice inside my head has been my own the whole time, pondered Cavanaugh, as the bus drove past him, barreling its way through the middle of town, uphill, then downhill, then back up the hill again.

Somewhere down the road, a sign glowed on and off.

Cavanaugh's Daughter Waits
for the Jingle and the Creak

She closed her bedroom door and waited for the sound of her father's footsteps coming up the staircase. She knew it would be days, possibly weeks, that she would hear the sound of his house keys jingling in his coat pocket as he walked up the stairs, but she was determined to keep the door shut until such a sound came, however long it took.

The jingle of his keys.

The creak of the stairs.

Sounds only a father could make after a long day at the office.

And what, exactly, did her father do in that office that he took the bus to every morning?

"I crunch numbers, angel, push pencils," he told her when she once had asked. "You know—the usual." She had not a clue what her father had meant by any of this, but she still remembered what he had told her regardless.

Her father felt ordinary to her—not heroic, like so many of her friends claimed their own fathers were—but his constant presence in her life was a comfort to her. He was never gone for days at a time like some of the other fathers were for their jobs. No matter how long his day was, and no matter how tired he sounded lumbering up the stairs, he always came home.

Until now.

She looked over at the bobblehead doll standing on the nightstand next to her bed—the one that had replaced the one given to her by her father.

Why in the world had he taken the latter one from her room, and why was he holding it when she saw him through the window? Was there something wrong with it? Was he showing it to someone at work? Was he going to get it autographed like one of those old baseballs he had in his closet? Was he ever even going to bring it back to her?

He *will* bring it back to me, she figured. For what would a grown man be doing carrying around a bobblehead doll in one hand and a briefcase full of very important papers in the other?

She laid herself back down on the bed, her eyes following the gliding shadows being made across her ceiling with each passing vehicle on the road, and listened and waited for the jingle and the creak to come.

Somewhere outside her window, a dog barked.

CAVANAUGH ASSESSES HIS FINGERS

IT WAS A FEW MINUTES past noon by the time Cavanaugh reached Wrong Way Corrigan's, its large neon sign not so much glowing on and off, he realized, as much as refracting the midday sunlight.

Cavanaugh considered the first two words of the sign as he stood in front of the entrance: WRONG WAY.

"No," he said aloud. "It's the *right* way."

With the bobblehead in one hand and his briefcase full of nothing in the other, Cavanaugh pushed open the doors, and was immediately greeted by the same ashy aroma he had encountered in his previous visit to Corrigan's.

Cavanaugh looked around.

No customers in the bar area.

No customers in the restaurant area.

No sign of the waitress.

No reason to stick around then, figured Cavanaugh.

He was about to turn around, when he heard a man's voice coming from one of the smoke-filled corners of the room.

"Can I help you, sir?"

Cavanaugh considered the question in the most general terms for a moment—*Could anyone help me at this point?*—before accepting the question for what it was.

After all, he was very hungry again, and also thirsty—*very* thirsty.

"I could use a drink."

"Excellent," said the man, as he emerged more clearly from out of the smoky haze. His arms were covered in tattoos—snakes, swords, skulls and the like. His hair was pony-tailed in the back and the glasses covering his eyes were the frameless kind—the trendy sort of ones that Cavanaugh used to wear when he was young and strong, like this man.

"Would you like to sit at the bar, sir?"

"You know what," said Cavanaugh, "I'm actually feeling kind of hungry as well. I'll take a booth, if you don't mind."

"Sure thing."

Cavanaugh followed the waiter to the booth. It was the same booth as the booth he sat in the previous time he was at Corrigan's.

"So, have you ever been here before, sir?"

Cavanaugh was about to come clean, but decided against it. After all, he had not been clean in any sense of the word for quite a few days, so why start now?

"Nope. Never been."

"Ah, well, welcome to Corrigan's. I will be your waiter this afternoon." The waiter handed Cavanaugh a menu, for the menus were not neatly stacked and leaning against the wall of the booth like last time. "Today's specials, as you'll see, are clipped to the second page there. Drinks are on the back. I'll be right back to take your order."

"Actually," said Cavanaugh, "I already know what I want."

"Great. What can I get for you?"

"The forty-for-forty."

"Sir?"

"You know—the buffalo wings. The bucket of buffalo wings?"

"Oh, right—you mean the forty-for-forty special. Well, that special is not on the menu today, unfortunately." The waiter looked at the bobblehead sitting next to Cavanaugh, as if seeing it for the first time. He then turned his gaze back toward Cavanaugh. "Say, I thought you said this was your first time here—how did you know about the special?"

Cavanaugh looked at the waiter.

The waiter looked at Cavanaugh.

"A friend," said Cavanaugh.

"A friend?"

"A friend told me. About the special. He came here once before and had it—said it was really good."

"Ah, of course. Well, I'll give you some more time to decide, and I'll be right back to take your order." The waiter was about to turn toward the kitchen, but Cavanaugh needed to get the ball rolling right away.

"A pitcher."

"What was that?" The waiter took a half-step closer to Cavanaugh's booth. "Did you say something?"

"Yeah, I said a pitcher."

"A pitcher?"

"Yeah, a pitcher. A pitcher of Guinness. I'll have that again."

"Did you say *again*?"

Cavanaugh looked at the waiter.

The waiter looked at Cavanaugh, as he stood over the table with his hands on his hips, waiting for his customer to reply.

This waiter, thought Cavanaugh. This waiter is good at waiting.

"Well, what I meant was . . ." Cavanaugh cleared his throat. "What I meant was that Guinness—it's a drink I order a lot. You know, like whenever I go out for a drink, I mean."

"Hmm, I see," said the waiter, nodding. "One pitcher of Guinness coming right up." He looked back more than once at Cavanaugh as he made his way behind the empty bar counter.

Cavanaugh looked right back. He was good at looking back.

He looked up at the TV screen. A cartoon was on. The one with the pigs with the British accents again.

Again.

Everything was again when it came to Cavanaugh.

The waiter came back again, this time with a full pitcher of beer in his hand.

"Here's your Guinness, sir. Have you decided on what to order yet?"

"No," said Cavanaugh. "I still need more time."

"Sure," said the waiter. "Take all the time you need." The waiter remained by the table, waiting, pen and pad in his hands, ready to write down the order when it came.

Cavanaugh picked at his ear with his finger. He could feel the flakes peeling off as he picked.

"You know what," said Cavanaugh, "I'll have the fingers."

"The chicken fingers, you mean?"

Something dangled from the rim of Cavanaugh's ear—it felt larger than just a flake. Cavanaugh yanked it off and flicked it without looking.

He looked up from the menu again, and saw the waiter still awaiting his response.

"Yeah," he said. "The chicken fingers. Two orders."

"Two orders?"

"Yes, that's what I said. Two orders."

"Two orders. One for each of you, right?" He nodded at the doll and winked at Cavanaugh.

Cavanaugh forced a smile. Different waiter, same joke. "Of course."

"So, who is that supposed to be?"

"Excuse me?"

"The bobblehead there—which player is that?"

"Oh, right," said Cavanaugh. "Um, no one in particular, I don't think. Got it at one of those minor league ballgames."

"Have you given it a name?"

Cavanaugh could not believe his ears. "A name?"

"Yeah, the bobblehead," said the waiter, pointing his pen at the doll. "Have you given it a name?"

Cavanaugh looked at the waiter.

The waiter looked at Cavanaugh.

Cavanaugh let him have it. "It's Kav . . ."

"Kav . . . ?"

"It's Brett. His name is Brett."

"Oh." The waiter smiled at Cavanaugh. "Actually, my nephew is named Brett."

Cavanaugh nodded his head, sipped his Guinness.

"Well, I'll be right back with your order," said the waiter. He looked up at the TV screen and saw the pigs with the British accents. "Oh, this episode is my favorite. Such a funny show—even for grown-ups."

Cavanaugh watched the waiter disappear into the kitchen and wondered to himself if there really was a chef back there, or if everything was just premade and microwaved. He took another sip of his Guinness, then blew out a deep breath. He felt his phone vibrate in his pocket but decided to let the call go to voicemail. When the vibrations came to an end, he pulled the phone out and looked at the digits.

It was Mrs. Cavanaugh.

He knew it: she missed him after all. And why wouldn't she, for their marriage counted for something, did it not?

Oh, Missus Cavanaugh! Missus Cavanaugh!

He could still feel her satin on his fingertips as he sipped.

What was going on with him right now—this was just temporary, he knew. He had been on the brink before and had overcome—he knew he could do it again.

"I *will* do it again," said Cavanaugh.

Cavanaugh looked up at the TV screen. The pigs were getting on a bus. Or maybe it was a train—it was hard to tell.

The pony-tailed waiter with the tats was back, this time with the food. He placed Cavanaugh's lunch on the table. "And here are your two orders of chicken fingers, sir."

Definitely microwaved, thought Cavanaugh, but he nodded in appreciation regardless. No one else on staff was helping this young fellow. It was the least he could do.

"Could I get you any honey mustard sauce with that, Mister Cavanaugh?"

Cavanaugh almost dropped his glass beer mug. "How—how do you know my name is Cavanaugh?"

"Um, well, you sort of just said it was, didn't you?"

"I did?"

"Uh-huh. You said, 'Cavanaugh looked up at the TV screen,' and then you looked up at the TV screen, so I figured that Cavanaugh had to be you. Am I wrong?"

"But how did you know I said that? How could you hear what was being said?"

"Um . . ." The waiter shrugged. "Because . . . you said it out loud?"

"Oh, um, I see, I—"

"And before that, too—you said, 'Cavanaugh looked at the waiter. The waiter looked at Cavanaugh.'"

"Dear god—"

"And you said I was good at waiting. I appreciate your saying that, by the way."

Cavanaugh slumped in his seat.

"Um, yes, I can see that, Mister Cavanaugh. You are, indeed, slumping in your seat."

"Good lord—I said that out loud, too?"

"Yup, you sure did, Mister Cavanaugh." The waiter leaned in and whispered. "Hey, man, are you tripping out on something, or what? Hit me up with that, will ya? I won't tell a soul."

The waiter leaned back and chuckled.

Cavanaugh scratched hard at the inside of his ear. Something in there was oozing. He took his finger out and assessed the crusty redness. He then inserted a different finger, pulled that one out as well, and compared samples.

"Mister Cavanaugh?"

Cavanaugh looked up from his fingers, and saw the waiter, his hands clasped together, waiting.

Cavanaugh looked up from his fingers—did I say that or did the voice say that? Cavanaugh was no longer sure of anything.

"Mister Cavanaugh, did you want that honey mustard with your chicken fingers, or are you all set?"

"Um . . ." Cavanaugh scratched his ear even harder. Something there was still dangling. "Sure. Honey mustard would be great. Thanks."

"No problem. I'll go grab some for you."

Cavanaugh looked up at the TV screen again. The bus had broken down. A pig in a mechanic's jumpsuit was under the hood, checking the engines, changing a tire.

The waiter returned.

"Here's your honey mustard. If you need anything else, let me know, okay?"

Cavanaugh nodded. He looked down at the honey mustard, a beige-yellow clump in a tiny plastic container. It made him think of the toilet in his motel room.

Cavanaugh pushed the honey mustard aside. He finished off the first round of beer, poured out a second, and began to eat. By the time he finished his second round, he had all but forgotten about the toilet in his motel room.

He looked down at the bobblehead sitting next to him.

Same old smirk.

Same old Kavanaugh.

O'REILLY SEES ANOTHER SIGN

EVERY TIME HE SAW Mrs. Cavanaugh's car whiz by his house from his living room window, he took it to be a sign from above. Then again, everything was a sign from above when it came to a man as desperate as O'Reilly.

Thus, when he limped down the road and stood at the foot of the driveway of the Cavanaugh house with his hair neatly combed and pasted against his broad forehead, a small beaten-up suitcase in one hand and a pink flower uprooted from his next-door neighbor's garden in the other, it made perfect sense to him that he would see the silhouette of Mrs. Cavanaugh shaking out her hair through the window shade of an upstairs window, for that, too, he concluded, had to be a sign from above. He half-expected the silhouette of Cavanaugh to appear through that same window as well, but then remembered his daughter telling him that the Cavanaugh girl, who had been absent from school for days now, had, prior to her absence, revealed that her father would be on the road for some time—for work, presumably— and would not be returning home for quite a while.

Or at least that was the story according to the Cavanaugh girl. It was a story that he, O'Reilly, was quite familiar with, for it was a re-curring one within his own household—a story that was more a cover story than the real story, which, O'Reilly sensed, was that something had gone awry within the Cavanaugh household, and that Cavanaugh, as many a husband and father were prone to do when overwhelmed by the challenges of family life, had either removed himself from the picture, or, as in his own case, been forcibly driven into exile.

But just as quickly as the silhouette of Mrs. Cavanaugh had appeared in the window, so too it had disappeared.

Perhaps that is a sign, too, he wondered. Or perhaps there were never any signs to begin with.

He was about to turn around and limp back up the road, when he saw another figure appear in a different upstairs window of the

Cavanaugh house. This figure was not a silhouette, but the freckled face of a small, red-haired child.

It was the Cavanaugh girl.

She was gazing out into the distance, to somewhere beyond the houses and trees that lined the streets of the neighborhood, perhaps toward the horizon, presumed O'Reilly, where the evening sky swallowed the sun whole. Her gaze stayed locked in its position for a while, then shifted downward, toward O'Reilly, her searching eyes meeting his own.

She waved her small hand at O'Reilly and smiled.

He waved his large hand at the Cavanaugh girl and smiled back.

A sign from above, indeed.

CAVANAUGH Y KAVANAUGH

WHEN HE WOKE UP, he was still in the booth, his head lying sideways across the tabletop, his pitcher empty, his plate licked clean, and, judging from the small slip of paper lying by the tip of his nose, the bill already paid in cash.

Next to his head, on the table, stood the bobblehead. Tinkering with the bobblehead was the waiter and a smaller man of darker complexion—a busboy, perhaps, figured Cavanaugh. They both stood over the table, pressing the button at the base of the bobblehead, trying to make its head bobble. Neither had any luck with it, but they broke into laughter regardless. Cavanaugh had the strong sense that they had been standing there, laughing, for quite some time.

"Guess the batteries have run out," said the waiter to the busboy.

"Sí," said the busboy. "Están agotadas. Sí."

They saw Cavanaugh lift his head.

The busboy spoke first, pointing his finger at the bobblehead: "Señor Kavanaugh, ¿sí?"

Cavanaugh leaned back against the booth and nodded. "Sí. Señor Kavanaugh. Sí." He held the paper receipt up to the light. Was that two pitchers or three pitchers he was reading? It was all too blurry to him.

The busboy lifted the bobblehead off the table, held it in the air, gave it a gentle shake, then nodded. "Señor Kavanaugh."

Cavanaugh nodded again. "Señor Kavanaugh."

The busboy pointed his finger at the bobblehead again. "Señor Kavanaugh." Then he pointed his finger at Cavanaugh. "Señor Cavanaugh, ¿sí?"

"Sí, yes, sí," said Cavanaugh. "I'm Cavanaugh, he's Kavanaugh. Sí."

The waiter elbowed the busboy, and they both erupted with laughter again. Cavanaugh could see tears coming out of the waiter's eyes.

"Cavanaugh y Kavanaugh," said the busboy. "¿Sí?"

"Sí," said the waiter. "Cavanaugh y Kavanaugh."

Cavanaugh shrugged. "Yup. There you have it. Cavanaugh and Kavanaugh. That's us."

"¡Cavanaugh y Kavanaugh!" cheered the busboy.

"¡Cavanaugh y Kavanaugh!" echoed the waiter.

"Sí, sí," said Cavanaugh. "Cavanaugh y Kavanaugh. Cavanaugh y Kavanaugh. Very funny. Muy cómico. Sí."

Cavanaugh waited for the laughter to subside, but instead it kept elevating.

The busboy was a brown man, but his face was now purple.

The waiter was a white man, but his face was now blue.

Cavanaugh picked at his ear: what came out was red and yellow.

He looked down at the table: something orange had oozed onto its surface where the side of his head had been.

Cavanaugh looked up at the screen: more pigs, more vehicles. It was a pig series marathon.

There was a sound of something being slammed shut in the background behind the waiter and the busboy—a door, perhaps.

Then, from somewhere in the smoky depths of the room, came a raspy voice. It was neither his own voice, nor the voice from inside his own head.

It was the voice of a woman.

"What the fuck are *you* doing here?" said the voice.

Cavanaugh recognized the voice right away despite its furious tone. It was the voice of the woman he had come to see: the waitress.

But Cavanaugh was beginning to have second thoughts.

He looked at the waiter.

He looked at the busboy.

They were no longer laughing.

"Sí, Señor Cavanaugh," whispered the busboy. "Nosotros ya no estamos riendo. No laugh. Sí."

He could barely see her at first, only hear her, her heeled boots clacking against the wood of the floor. Something about her jingled, but Cavanaugh could not tell what it was.

Belt against buckle.

Boot against wood.

When she emerged into full view, it almost felt to Cavanaugh that the smoke had been her own all along—as if she had been watching the three of them from some shadowy corner of the room, waiting for her moment to pounce, the smoke a byproduct of her simmering ire.

She flicked something onto the floor, then stamped it out with her foot. Her eyes were bulging and her cheeks were red with rage.

But still not a trace of makeup.

She leaned over the table, and got right in Cavanaugh's face. "What did you just say to me?"

"I, uh, I, um . . ." He could see this woman had suffered. From his transgression, undoubtedly, but surely from the transgressions of other men as well.

"But still not a trace of makeup? Is that what you just said to me? But still not a trace of makeup?"

She looked back at the waiter, then back at the busboy, the latter still holding the bobblehead in his hands.

She grabbed the bobblehead from the busboy, inspected it for herself.

"Yep," she said. "That's the one. That's the doll." She looked back toward Cavanaugh. "And that's the guy. The guy who followed me into the ladies' restroom a couple of weeks ago."

A couple of weeks ago? Cavanaugh suddenly wondered how many days, exactly, was it that he had been off the grid.

The waiter looked at Cavanaugh, then back at the waitress. "Wait a minute—*he's* the one? *He's* the guy?"

"Yup," said the waitress. "He's the one. The *guy.*"

Both the waiter and the busboy, their fists clenched, took a step toward Cavanaugh, but the waitress put her hand out to stop them.

"It's okay, fellas," said the waitress. "I got this."

She looked at the bobblehead again. Then back at Cavanaugh.

"So, Cavanaugh, you never told me: Who's this doll supposed to be?"

"Ese es el juez Kavanaugh, señorita," said the busboy.

"I'm asking Cavanaugh," said the waitress, holding up a hand, her gaze still fixed on Cavanaugh. "So, tell me, Cavanaugh, who is he?"

Cavanaugh looked over at the busboy. Then at the waiter. Then back at the waitress.

"It's him, alright," said Cavanaugh. "It's Kavanaugh."

"Kavanaugh, eh? Kavanaugh, as in *Brett* Kavanaugh?"

"Sí," said Cavanaugh.

"What was that, Cavanaugh?"

"I mean, yes—Brett Kavanaugh. The doll—it's him."

The waitress turned her attention back to the bobblehead, tilting it to one side, then the other, and then placed it back down on the table.

She pressed the button on its base. The doll did not budge.

She looked at Cavanaugh.

She looked at the waiter.

She looked at the busboy.

Then she looked back at Cavanaugh.

In a sudden burst of fury, she growled, gnashed her teeth, and grabbed the bobblehead off the table by its arms with both her hands before raising it straight up over her head. Seeing her on the cusp of slamming the bobblehead down on the table and smashing it to pieces, Cavanaugh screamed.

"Please! Please! Don't do it! Don't do it! It's my daughter's! It's my daughter's! Oh, christ, please, please don't do it!"

The muscles on the face of the waitress suddenly went lax. She looked at Cavanaugh. There was pity in her eyes—whether it was for him or for his daughter, or for her own situation, he was uncertain.

She looked at the waiter.

She looked at the busboy.

Then she looked back at Cavanaugh.

All of this looking made Cavanaugh all the more dizzy.

"Yes, Cavanaugh, I *am* looking back at you," said the waitress. "And all of this looking around is making *me* quite dizzy as well."

She placed the bobblehead back on the table.

"Look," said Cavanaugh, "the reason I came here was . . . was . . ." He was not sure how to continue, but continue he did: "The reason why I came here—why I came here *again*—was to apologize to you. The police officer—he came to my motel room and told me all about what I had done. I swear, I don't remember it—*any* of it—but I apologize nonetheless. That is, I mean, I think I blacked out. But I believe you—I believe your story. This doll—this Brett Kavanaugh bobble-head doll—it deserves to be smashed to pieces, but my daughter— well, she has no idea who Brett Kavanaugh even is—not yet, anyway— and I'm just thinking it's *me* you're mad at anyway, right? It's *me* you're mad at, not my daughter's doll, so let's leave her and the doll out of it, okay? This doll—this stupid, stupid, stupid doll—I don't know why I'm still carrying it around. But it's been with me for days, if not weeks, now. It belongs with my daughter, but instead it's with me. The truth is I've been away from home a very long time now—or at least it feels like a very long time—and I don't know when I'll be coming back. But this doll—this doll has been good company for me, and it makes me think of my little daughter whenever I see it. It makes me think of her and what I am to her, and reminds me that at some point, at some time, when I am no longer the way I am right now, I will come back to her—to her, to her mother, to our home, and that we—the three of us—will be the happy family we once were all over again. I don't know when exactly that will be, but for now, this doll—this doll right here—it's what's going to bring me back to my little girl, my little an- gel, for this doll is her doll, and I am going to bring it back home—I swear, I swear with all my heart I will, amen."

The waitress said nothing at first—just stared at Cavanaugh. The corner of her eyes looked moist to him, but he figured that was per- haps just the light.

She looked at the waiter.

She looked at the busboy.

She looked back at Cavanaugh.

She waited in silence for a few moments, perhaps more. She was good at waiting.

"I *was* good at waiting," said the waitress. "And I still am."

"You are indeed," said Cavanaugh.

"Alright. So, let me get this straight, Cavanaugh, because I'm trying to wrap my head around it." She leaned in toward him again. "You bought a Brett Kavanaugh bobblehead doll for your *daughter*?"

"Yes," said Cavanaugh. "Yes, I did. I mean, I had to, I—"

"You *had* to? You *had* to buy a Brett Kavanaugh bobblehead doll for your *daughter*?"

"Well, um, yeah, I had to. Everyone was buying one—the whole stadium. Even O'Reilly—"

"Oh, yeah—that O'Reilly guy again. By the way, who the fuck *is* O'Reilly anyway? You know, I kept hearing you say his name the last time you were sitting in this booth. Who the heck is he?"

Cavanaugh looked up at the waitress.

Then at the waiter.

Then at the busboy.

Then back at the waitress.

"Um, well, O'Reilly, he's my—well, actually, to tell you the truth, I'm not really sure who O'Reilly is. At first I thought he was the opposite of me, but now I think he sort of *is* me, or at least the man I used to be, I—"

"Cavanaugh, Cavanaugh," said the waitress. "Hold on a minute here, okay?"

"What?" said Cavanaugh. "What's the matter? What's wrong?"

"What's wrong? You're asking me what's wrong, Cavanaugh?"

Cavanaugh. Only two women had ever called him by that name in his whole life, and the waitress was one of them.

This is a nice woman, a good woman, thought Cavanaugh. Did she hear him say *that*, too? He was not certain, but if she had heard it, so be it, he felt.

She put a firm hand on his shoulder.

"Look, Cavanaugh," she said. "I don't know what's ailing you, but here's what I do know: you need to get yourself some help."

"Help? What kind of help? You mean help for my head?"

"Uh-huh."

"You know, my head hasn't always bobbled around like this. It's just something that started happening after I—"

"No, Cavanaugh. I don't mean that kind of help for your head. I mean the mental kind of help. Psychological help. *That* kind of help."

"Oh, um, right," said Cavanaugh. "*That* kind of help."

"I mean, it's not your fault, Cavanaugh. Sounds like you were probably a normal guy at one point, and then—bam!" She slammed the table with her fist. "You went a little crazy."

Cavanaugh nodded. "Yeah, well, that's kind of what happened. The doll—"

"The doll? The *doll*? You mean *this* doll?" She held the bobblehead up with one hand around its neck for a moment then put it right back down. "This doll's got nothing to do with it. It's *that*." She pressed the tip of her finger against his head. "It's whatever is going on in there— *that* is what it's all got to do with—whatever *that* is, that's what it's got to do with."

Cavanaugh gulped. "And what—and what do you think *that* is?"

"How the fuck should I know, Cavanaugh? That's why you should go get some help."

"You mean, the mental kind of help, right?"

"Yeah, Cavanaugh. The mental kind of help."

She took a napkin off the table and dabbed at the honey mustard at the corner of his mouth. She looked over her shoulder at her two co-workers, who were still listening in, rolled her eyes, and then looked back at Cavanaugh.

"Come on, Cavanaugh. Let's go get you on a bus to where you need to go. You like buses, right?"

Cavanaugh nodded.

The waiter and the busboy each took one arm and lifted him up gently out of the booth.

"Vamos, Señor Cavanaugh," muttered the busboy.

"Say," said Cavanaugh to the waitress, as they escorted him toward the door, "I never got your name."

But before he even had a chance to hear her say it, Cavanaugh had already been nudged out of Corrigan's, out into the breezy and bitter air, his bobblehead doll in one hand, his briefcase full of nothing in the other, the waiter and the busboy towing him across the road to where the next bus would pick him up and take him to wherever it may happen to go next.

Somewhere along the way, a dog barked.

CAVANAUGH RECEIVES ANOTHER WAKE-UP CALL

Didn't you hear me the first time?

I said wake up!

Wake up, little boy!

You better wake up now, little boy, or you'll miss your stop!

And if you miss your stop who knows where you'll end up!

Down the hill—that's where you'll end up!

Down the hill, then up the hill, then down again!

Because you're a Cavanaugh, you silly boy!

Because you're a Cavanaugh, and that's where all Cavanaughs end up: down the hill!

Up the hill, then down the hill, then down, down, down!

Because you're a Cavanaugh!

Because you're a pencil-pusher!

Because you're a number-cruncher!

Because you're a middling, middle-aged middleman!

Because you're a silly, silly, silly, silly, silly-dilly boy who never wakes up when he's supposed to wake up!

If only you were more like your friend Brett.

THE OFFICER CANNOT BELIEVE HIS EARS

Yeah, this is Blue Dog Three. I'm at the ballgame with my boy—what's up?

Cavanaugh did *what*?

He said *what*?

You're joking, right?

Alright, stay there. I'm on my way.

CAVANAUGH SITS NEXT TO THE LORD

THEY HAD PUT HIM on the wrong bus, but Cavanaugh did not realize it until he had opened his eyes and found his face pressed against the glass of the window. He had wanted them to put him on the bus headed to his favorite bodega—the one with the anonymous voice behind the counter—but this bus was headed in the opposite direction.

This bus, Cavanaugh knew, was headed for home.

He looked at his phone to see the time.

Five thirty-three.

Rush hour.

No wonder the bus was so crowded.

A passenger was seating in the seat next to him—a man.

Or was it a woman?

A newspaper was blocking the passenger's face, so there was no way for Cavanaugh to know. He tried to lean this way and that, but he could not get a good look.

Cavanaugh cleared his throat, then spoke: "My, this sure is a crowded bus, ain't it?"

He waited for the passenger to reply, but he was only met with silence.

Cavanaugh tried again: "I said this sure is a crowded bus, ain't it?"

The passenger turned the page, but otherwise the newspaper did not budge from its position, and the passenger still offered no reply.

The bus went over a bump and something jingled.

It was the passenger—or something that was on the passenger, figured Cavanaugh—that jingled.

The bus went over another bump, then another, and the jingling sound continued.

Jingle-jingle.

Jingle-jingle.

Passengers got on the bus.

Passengers got off the bus.

The passenger with the newspaper remained in his seat next to Cavanaugh, as if frozen in place.

The bus resumed its route, uphill, then downhill, then back up the hill again.

Bump, bump, bump went the bus.

Jingle, jingle, jingle went the passenger with the newspaper.

Cavanaugh looked at the top of the newspaper's front page, which was facing him, and found the date of the paper's publication. The date stunned him: it had been almost three weeks since he had left home, and a new season had already begun.

How long was I hiding in my office? wondered Cavanaugh. And how long was I in that motel room? He had no recollection of either his arrival at or departure from the latter, let alone paying for his stay.

He studied the passenger's fingers gripping the paper. They were covered in gloves that were black, and thus offered Cavanaugh no clues.

Cavanaugh returned his gaze toward the window, and, with the bobblehead doll and briefcase full of nothing both on his lap, watched the houses as they rolled by, a pumpkin on almost every front stoop. All the while, the bus hummed along, uphill, then downhill, then back up the hill again, its brakes screeching at every stop.

Bump, bump.

Jingle, jingle.

Who was this passenger?

And why was this passenger's face concealed in the manner it was concealed?

And why, Cavanaugh wondered, did it matter so much to him?

But Cavanaugh knew why: it was because of that damn jingling sound.

Belt against buckle.

Boot against—Cavanaugh looked down toward the floor of the bus, studied the passenger's footwear.

It was footwear larger than his own footwear, a pair of work boots that he was more than a little familiar with.

Bump, bump.

Jingle, jingle.

And then, as if struck by a lightning bolt, Cavanaugh had suddenly solved the mystery: it was him—the janitor from his office, the man from the motel.

It was Brett. It *had* to be.

"Brett," said Cavanaugh. He waited for a reaction, a slight crinkling of the paper perhaps, but there was no reply.

He said it louder: "Brett." He saw one of the fingers bend for a moment, but then a page was turned and nothing more.

But this did not deter Cavanaugh. He just knew it had to be him, the man with the jingle, the lord of the keys.

He looked around the bus, then back at the mysterious passenger. He cupped his hands over his mouth, and let it rip.

"Yes, god, oh, yes, god, oh, yes, god, oh!" he shouted.

No response.

"Fuck me, fuck me, fuck me!"

Another passenger, an old woman with white hair and bifocals, sneered at Cavanaugh, then looked away, but the passenger with the newspaper remained concealed.

Cavanaugh cleared his throat, then continued: "Please come, please come, please come!"

A page was turned, then another, but nothing more.

Cavanaugh sighed and buried his face into his lap, his head bumping up against the bobblehead, as the bus bobbled along.

But then Cavanaugh's head suddenly shot up from his hands. "I got it," he said. "This *has* to work."

He turned his head and glanced at the jingling passenger, then looked downward at what had been sitting on his lap the whole ride: the bobblehead doll.

He pressed the button down on the base of the bobblehead, but the bobblehead would not bobble. He had almost forgotten: the batteries had run out at Corrigan's.

Cavanaugh pressed on regardless, but, still, the bobblehead would not budge. He pressed down again and again, shaking it now and then before he pressed—but still, there was no sign of movement.

Cavanaugh then had an idea, one that had worked for him before in similar situations.

He opened the battery hatch, and swapped the placement of the two batteries—the one on the left went to the right, the one on the right went to the left.

He reclosed the hatch and took a deep breath. He then pressed down on the button at the base of the bobblehead and watched as the doll began to bobble.

The laughter came quickly from the passenger sitting next to him. It was a man's laughter, for sure. It was the same wheezy and snorty laughter Cavanaugh had heard in his cubicle when he was hiding under his desk.

The idea had worked.

So, I guess it really *is* him, figured Cavanaugh. It's *Brett.*

Cavanaugh watched the passenger jerk back and forth, back and forth, the newspaper never shifting from its position, the man's body convulsing in rhythm to the snapping sound of the bobblehead.

Bump, bump.

Jingle, jingle.

Snap, snap.

Belt against buckle.

Boot against wood.

Cavanaugh pressed the button down again.

And again.

And again.

Passengers got off the bus.

Passengers got on the bus.

Uphill and downhill.

Downhill and uphill.

Somewhere along the way, a dog barked.

Cavanaugh kept on pressing regardless.

CAVANAUGH HEARS AN ANGEL

WHEN HE GOT OFF the bus at his neighborhood stop, Cavanaugh decided to wait there for the next bus going in the opposite direction—back toward his favorite bodega.

"I could use a drink," said Cavanaugh.

He listened for the voice inside his head to respond in kind, but it was no longer lingering about on the inside—no, it was now projecting itself outward into the outside world, becoming his *own* speaking voice, hijacking his being, his very essence.

Standing under the light of a streetlamp, Cavanaugh placed his briefcase full of nothing down on the pavement, took out his phone, and checked the time again.

Six minutes after six.

He could see he had one new voice message, then remembered how his phone had vibrated in his pocket at Corrigan's.

Cavanaugh read the name above the digits: Mrs. Cavanaugh. Even on his phone, she was Mrs. Cavanaugh to him.

He pressed play and held the phone to his ear.

But it was not Mrs. Cavanaugh—it was Cavanaugh's daughter.

"Daddy? It's me. Please come home. I'm calling you from Mommy's phone, but she doesn't know I'm calling you, so please don't tell her I called. Okay? But Daddy, um . . . Daddy, please come home. Just please come home. I miss you, Daddy. I miss you so much, okay, so please come home. I miss you very, very, very, very much. And also, um . . . Daddy, do you still have my bobblehead doll? Mommy said you were getting my bobblehead doll fixed at the store and that's why you were holding it when I saw you in the window. So, if you still have it, please bring it home, okay? Mister O'Reilly gave me the same bobblehead doll while you were away, but he now says I have to give it back to him because he said it's really his daughter's, okay? Okay, Daddy? Please come home, okay? Please come home and bring me back my bobblehead doll. Okay, Daddy? Okay, Daddy. I'll see you soon. I love you. Bye."

Cavanaugh pulled the phone from his ear. He scrolled back to the message, pressed play, and listened again.

Daddy?

It's me.

Please come home.

Cavanaugh felt a tear run down his cheek, then another.

He pressed play again.

Daddy, please come home.

Just please come home.

I miss you, Daddy.

I miss you so much, okay, so please come home.

I miss you very, very, very, very much.

Cavanaugh tilted his head back and wailed to the glowing streetlamp above.

He pressed play again.

Okay, Daddy?

Okay, Daddy.

I'll see you soon.

I love you.

Bye.

A bus arrived at the stop and the doors swung open, but Cavanaugh would not board it.

He pressed play again, and remained there, weeping under the light of the streetlamp, listening to the recorded voice of his little angel.

Another bus came, another bus went.

He pressed play again.

There Cavanaugh stood, a middling, middle-aged middleman, sobbing in the middle of the street, in the middle of his home neighborhood, his head bobbling up and down against the ebb and flow of the evening wind, a phone in one hand, a bobblehead doll in the other, his briefcase full of nothing on the pavement at his feet.

Somewhere down the road, a garage door opened.
He pressed play again.
Somewhere down the road, a robin sang its evening song.
He pressed play again.
Somewhere down the road, a dog barked.
He pressed play again.

BLUE DOG THREE TEN–FOURS A TEN–TEN

Blue Dog Three, this is Red Dog Seven. We got a possible ten-ten at the bodega on Main. Do you copy?

"Red Dog Seven. This is Blue Dog Three. Ten-four on your ten-ten. Is the suspect armed? Over. "

Affirmative, Blue Dog Three. Suspect is holding a briefcase in one hand, and a bobblehead doll in the other. Over.

"Ah, well, we all know who that is, Red Dog Seven. Over."

Roger that, Blue Dog Three. Should I send you some backup?

"Backup?"

For the ten-ten. Over.

"Negatory on the backup, Red Dog Seven. Think I got this covered."

Roger that, Blue Dog Three. But watch that briefcase, ya hear? Could be something in it this time. Over.

"I'll be sure to keep my eye on it, Red Dog Seven. Thanks for the tip. Over and out."

CAVANAUGH IS THURSDAY AND HUNGARY

Eye cood yooz uh drink. Eye cood booz uh drink. Eye cood wood shood uh drink. Eye cood drink uh drink on uh rinka. Eye cood drink uh rinka on uh dinka. Eye uh eye uh eye um can eye have uh drinka? Uh drinka rinka on a stinka? Eye yoosta drink and drink and drink wen eye yoosta drink wen eye wuz uh drunka. Wut om sayin iz om drunk four uh drink iz wut om sayin heera.

Hay man r u brett ore r u bret? R u Cavanawwww ore r u Ka-vanananawwwwwwww?

Witch izit?

Tel mee.

Fok u.

U hurd me.

Eye sed fffffahhhhg. U.

Om Thursday ear uhghen iz wut om say yin ear.

Thursday n Hungary.

Letz git bak onda bus anda orda sumtin inn oh k.

Oh k.

The Voice Behind the Counter
Voices His Concern

HE WAS JUST IN HERE a minute ago, Officer—you just missed him. Comes in here like every other day now, no matter the hour.

Nine AM.

Ten AM.

Eleven AM.

Noon.

Happy hour.

After-hours.

Any hour, makes no difference.

This customer—he calls himself Cavanaugh, with a C. And the only reason I know it's a C and not a K is because that's what he says it is whenever he's in conversation with himself, which is the all the time when it comes to him.

Cavanaugh this.

Cavanaugh that.

Missus Cavanaugh.

Cavanaugh's daughter.

Cavanaugh's daughter's teacher.

Everything's Cavanaugh when it comes to this Cavanaugh fella.

This Cavanaugh fella—he even said to me one time that he has a voice living and breathing inside his own head, and that this voice that is living and breathing inside his own head calls him Cavanaugh.

He actually said that to me—I swear.

He also said that this voice of his inside his own head reminded him of me and my own voice. Said he could hear them both but couldn't see who was behind them, whatever the hell that meant. Rest assured, I never did ask him what that meant, no sir. Figure the less questions I ask the better when it comes to this Cavanaugh fella. Just let him buy his beer and get the hell out, if you know what I mean.

But he has never stolen from me—not even under the influence has he ever tried to sneak one out on me. He's always been on the up-and-up, yessir.

But going back to the purpose of my calling you down here—well, it ain't to report a shoplifting of sorts, I can tell you that. This Cavanaugh fella—he ain't shoplifting on me none, no sir. It's just that I'm starting to feel a little—hmm, what's the word?—anxious around him. Anxious and edgy. And it's not just because he keeps coming in here taking up all my beer, for god knows I can use the business. But with all that beer he's getting from my shop—well, I just don't feel right about it, you see. Hurts just to see him stumble on in here the way he does with that same filthy shirt he's got on him and that same wet pair of pants of his, reeking up the whole shop, scratching away at his you-know-what like there ain't no tomorrow, and then watching him lumber on out with the very thing that's making it all worse for him.

I asked him one time if he drove at all, because that would be the final straw for me—I don't want my shop to be the source of any drunk drivers on the road—but he said that he never drives, that he only takes the bus, and that Missus Cavanaugh—his wife, I reckon—well, she's the driver of them two, or at least that's how he put it to me anyways.

But anyhow, I guess what I'm saying here is that I'm just a bit concerned about this Cavanaugh fella, and I don't want no trouble here—not for Cavanaugh, and certainly not for my shop. But if you could have one of your folks come by once in a while—you know, to sort of assess the situation?—well, I'd appreciate that very much, yessir.

At any rate, that's all I have to say about it. Sounds like you already know about that briefcase of his and that bobblehead he's always got with him, so I guess I won't bore you with any of the particulars on that.

Anyhow, feel free to help yourself to one or more of them doughnuts on the rack there, if you like. Made them myself from scratch behind the counter here. I'd offer you up some free coffee as well, but my machine here—well, it's fried-up pretty good at the moment. Something wrong with it way in the back of it, so it's hard to get a good look.

Say, I don't suppose you have one of them small flashlights on you now, do ya? Or was that something else I heard jingling about on your holster there?

Cavanaugh in a Vacuum

CAVANAUGH WOKE UP on the bus again, his mouth tasting of beer.

He could not remember boarding the bus, nor could he remember consuming any beer, but there he was again, the side of his head slumped against the window, thumping up against the glass. Next to him sat the bobblehead doll, and leaning against his leg on the floor was his briefcase full of nothing.

Hanging from the edge of his briefcase was a congealed morsel of sorts, peach-like and half-digested. He tried flicking it away with his foot, but the morsel latched on to the tip of his shoe and stayed there.

"Give it up," said the voice.

"I already have," said Cavanaugh.

The voice had detached itself, become separate from his own again—or had it?

Perhaps it is just me again conversing with myself, wondered Cavanaugh.

He peered out the window: it was pitch-black, too dark to see. It was dark inside the bus as well—just a small beam of dim light lit the interior. He surveyed the seats from where he sat and spotted no other passengers on the bus.

Other than the Kavanaugh doll, that is, thought Cavanaugh.

He stood the Kavanaugh doll on his lap, and pressed the button.

The doll did not budge. The batteries had gone dead again.

Cavanaugh wondered what time it was. He pulled out his phone from his coat, and pressed down on the home button: the phone had gone dead again as well.

Dead doll, dead phone.

He looked out the window again, into the blackness, and heard the drizzling rain tapping against the glass, barely detectable.

How long had it been since the last time he was on the bus? Was it now the same night, only hours later, he wondered, or was it now the next night? Or was it now already the next night after that next night?

This particular blackout from which he had now arisen unnerved him more than the others he had had in the past. He felt rudderless, in a vacuum, on a vehicle lost in time and space.

Jingle-jingle.

Jingle-jingle.

What was that?

Cavanaugh looked around, saw nothing—just the back of the bus driver's head. It was a head he had not seen before. Perhaps it was a head with something loose inside, imagined Cavanaugh, like a tiny metal object jingling about its interior.

Jingle-jingle.

Jingle-jingle.

No, it was not coming from up inside the head of the driver—it was coming from down much closer.

Jingle-jingle.

Jingle-jingle.

He looked down at his coat, reached into his pocket, felt around with his fingers.

Jingle-jingle.

Jingle-jingle.

He came across something small and metallic. He pulled it out.

Jingle-jingle.

Jingle-jingle.

The keys—for the house. For *his* house. But *was* it still his house?

Cavanaugh was uncertain. He shoved the keys back in his coat pocket.

I could use a drink.

The bus screeched and came to a halt.

The driver announced the cross street: it was Cavanaugh's neighborhood stop.

Cavanaugh peered out the window again, but recognized nothing in the darkness.

Wherever this bus had come from, and no matter how and when he had gotten on it, Cavanaugh knew he had come full circle.

The driver announced the cross street of the stop again, but for reasons Cavanaugh could not discern, the name of the cross street sounded different coming from this particular driver's mouth: it sounded robotic to Cavanaugh, droid-like, unhuman.

Cavanaugh picked the bobblehead up, grabbed his briefcase, and headed down the aisle, toward the front door. When he reached the driver's seat, he tried to catch a glimpse of the driver, but it was hard to see most of his face through all that shadow.

Cavanaugh could see the driver's mouth though—it was closed shut—and when the driver repeated the cross street of the station, it remained closed.

Cavanaugh tried to get a closer look, but no matter the angle from which he stood, the shadow over the driver's face was impenetrable.

The driver repeated the cross street again, a ventriloquist in the dark.

How could he announce all the stops like that without moving his mouth? wondered Cavanaugh. Was it an automated audio recording of some kind?

The driver repeated the cross street yet again, louder this time.

Then again, even louder.

Then again, louder still, straining Cavanaugh's eardrums.

Cavanaugh heard another jingling sound, but knew it was not coming from his keys this time.

"Stop!" shouted Cavanaugh. "Stop saying the stop!"

The driver repeated the stop again and again, the volume of his voice rising with each repetition.

Jingle-jingle.

Jingle-jingle.

Cavanaugh dropped the bobblehead and the briefcase on the floor and was on his knees next to the driver's seat. He covered his ears with his hands, but could not block out the piercing sound of the driver's voice. The driver's voice boomed louder and louder, the syllables of the cross street becoming more mangled, more distorted with every utterance, yet the driver's mouth remained frozen in place.

Impossible, thought Cavanaugh. Impossible!

Jingle-jingle.

Jingle-jingle.

Cavanaugh reached for the driver's shirt, tugged it toward him.

The driver's lips remained stuck together.

Jingle-jingle.

Jingle-jingle.

With a clump of shirt in his fist, Cavanaugh shook the driver, but the driver would not stop announcing the stop.

Jingle-jingle.

Jingle-jingle.

Cavanaugh spotted a name sewn into the driver's shirt, right above the chest pocket, and read it aloud: "Brett."

Jingle-jingle.

Jingle-jingle.

"No! No! It can't be! It can't be!"

Jingle-jingle.

Jingle-jingle.

"Brett!" screamed Cavanaugh. "Brett!"

Jingle-jingle.

Jingle-jingle.

Cavanaugh reached his hand out toward the shadow and thrust his fingers at the driver's lips, but the driver's mouth would not budge.

The driver announced the cross street again, a clattering of syllables, a screeching of soundwaves.

Jingle-jingle.

Jingle-jingle.

Cavanaugh pushed his fingers between the driver's lips, and burrowed his way in, felt his way around the wetness.

Jingle-jingle.

Jingle-jingle.

The name of the cross street filled his ears, consumed them, became them, was them.

Jingle-jingle.

Jingle-jingle.

Cavanaugh tugged once, then twice, then yanked as hard as he could, his fingers gripping onto a jagged object somewhere deep.

Jingle-jingle.

Jingle-jingle.

The name of the cross street was repeated again.

And again.

And again.

Cavanaugh held the object up to the dim beam of light, felt its serrations in his grasp.

Jingle-jingle.

Jingle-jingle.

Cavanaugh inspected the object for a brief moment, and despite it being difficult for him to see anything inside the bus, it did not take him long to identify what the object was.

Jingle-jingle.

Jingle-jingle.

"Dentures!" screamed Cavanaugh.

Jingle-jingle.

Jingle-jingle.

Cavanaugh dropped the dentures to the floor in horror and grabbed his ears. The blaring soundwaves had ceased, but he could still hear the call for the cross street, the syllables now clearer, more distinct to his ears. He rose from the floor of the bus and got one last glimpse of the driver whose jawline now had a deflated look to it, the jowls all in a droop.

But despite its change in appearance, the driver's mouth remained shut.

Cavanaugh now knew: it was not the driver that had been calling out the cross street—it was the voice inside his own head that been doing the calling.

Jingle-jingle.

Jingle-jingle.

Cavanaugh picked up the doll and briefcase from the floor and scurried off the bus. He ran as fast as he could for two or three blocks and then stopped to catch his breath, a slow and steady drizzle pelting down on the barren parts of his scalp. The gentle rain reminded him that he had not showered in days—weeks, even.

Cavanaugh looked up and down the road and saw no one—not even a shadow—but the voice had gotten it right: the cross street and neighborhood were indeed his own.

Things around him slowly began to feel familiar again—and sound familiar, too.

Somewhere down the road, a wind chime chimed.

Somewhere down the road, a train whistle whistled.

Somewhere down the road, a lone dog barked.

Cavanaugh followed the sounds, his keys jingling freely again inside his coat pocket, his house somewhere in the distance, his ordinary figure making extraordinary shadows against the pavement under the moonlight.

Cavanaugh Misses O'Reilly

Cavanaugh had not planned on stopping by the O'Reilly home, but he could see from the sidewalk on which he stood that some lights were on inside the house, the TV screen in their family room once again aglow in the background.

He was not sure what he wanted to say to O'Reilly. Would he admonish O'Reilly for shadowing him at work and at home? Or would he thank O'Reilly for his act of generosity toward his daughter despite the blatant passive-aggression behind the act? Or would he perhaps just congratulate him on his decision to quit drinking and recommit to his family and leave it at that?

Should he confront him, should he engage with him, or should he just simply say he was passing by and shake his hand?

Cavanaugh was not certain about what he was about to say or do, but rang the doorbell regardless.

Somewhere inside the house, a cat meowed.

A few moments later, he heard the sound of a lock being jiggled with from within.

The door swung open and a young girl stood in the doorway: it was the O'Reilly girl. She was wearing pink pajamas with yellow flowers on them.

"Hi," said Cavanaugh.

"Mister Cavanaugh? Is that you?"

"Well, uh . . . yeah. It is."

"You look sort of, um . . . different."

"Really? How so?"

"Well, your head, I mean. It's sort of—"

"Honey, who are you talking to?" It was a voice coming from beyond where the O'Reilly girl stood. A female voice. A grown-up voice. A breathy, soothing voice. "Did you ask who it was before you opened the door?"

"It's Mister Cavanaugh, Mom. From down the block." She looked back at Cavanaugh. "Hey, why are you holding that Brett doll, Mister Cavanaugh? Is that mine? I've been looking all over for it."

Cavanaugh was about to respond, when a woman wearing a two-piece cream-colored satin nightgown tied at the center appeared at the doorway, inserting herself next to the O'Reilly girl, a lit cigarette between her long, elegant fingers.

It was O'Reilly's wife, Mrs. O'Reilly. Cavanaugh had never formally met her before, but had seen her taking out the trash sometimes on his way to the bus stop. She was blonde and slender with slight curves and, Cavanaugh surmised, more than a few years younger than O'Reilly.

The woman took a drag and blew out.

Cavanaugh loved satin, even on women who smoked cigarettes.

"Missus O'Reilly? Hi, I'm—"

"I know who you are," said Mrs. O'Reilly. She took another puff and blew out again. "You're that Cavanaugh fella O'Reilly keeps telling me about."

Hmm, *O'Reilly*, thought Cavanaugh. She calls her husband by her last name—just like Mrs. Cavanaugh calls me by my last name.

He wondered, though: Did O'Reilly think of his wife as Mrs. O'Reilly just as he thought of his own wife as Mrs. Cavanaugh?

Mrs. O'Reilly smiled at Cavanaugh, but then the smile quickly faded. "Hey, are you here to see O'Reilly? Because O'Reilly—he hasn't been here for a few days or so. But he should be back here soon, I imagine."

"Oh," said Cavanaugh. "I see."

"Yeah," said Mrs. O'Reilly. "He does that every now and then." She looked down at her daughter and caressed her hair. "Right, love?"

The O'Reilly girl nodded.

Cavanaugh smiled at the O'Reilly girl.

"What was that you said?" said Mrs. O'Reilly.

"Um, I don't know," said Cavanaugh. "Did I say something?"

"Yeah," said Mrs. O'Reilly. "You just said, 'Cavanaugh smiled at the O'Reilly girl.'"

"I did?"

Mrs. O'Reilly nodded.

"Are you sure?"

Mrs. O'Reilly nodded again.

The O'Reilly girl nodded as well.

"Well, then I guess I must've. Sorry about that."

"Mister Cavanaugh?" said the O'Reilly girl.

Cavanaugh looked at the O'Reilly girl. To him, she did not look like either O'Reilly or Mrs. O'Reilly. Perhaps she was adopted, he wondered.

"Yes?"

"Is that Brett doll for me?"

Cavanaugh looked down at the Kavanaugh doll in the crook of his arm. While it was not intended for the O'Reilly girl but rather his own little girl, he held it out to her anyway, finding himself unable to resist either the young girl's charms or her satin-clad mother's inviting personality.

Besides, he figured the two young girls could always swap bobble-heads later, if they wished.

"Yes, it is for you," said Cavanaugh. "Think it needs new batteries though."

"Well, um—that was very sweet of you, Cavanaugh," said Mrs. O'Reilly. "What do you say, love?"

The young girl hugged the bobblehead against her cheek, and gave it a peck on the head. "Thank you, Mister Cavanaugh."

"Thanks, Cavanaugh," said Mrs. O'Reilly.

"My pleasure, Missus O'Reilly," said Cavanaugh.

Cavanaugh looked at Mrs. O'Reilly.

Mrs. O'Reilly looked at Cavanaugh.

The O'Reilly girl looked at Cavanaugh, then at Mrs. O'Reilly.

Mrs. O'Reilly took another drag and blew out.

"So," said Mrs. O'Reilly. "Guess it's getting late." She looked at her daughter. "Time for bed, love."

"Ugh, alright," said the O'Reilly girl. "Good night, Mister Cavanaugh."

"Good night," said Cavanaugh.

"Good night, Cavanaugh," said Mrs. O'Reilly.

"Good night, Missus O'Reilly," said Cavanaugh.

Mrs. O'Reilly was about to close the door, but the O'Reilly girl was not finished yet.

"Mister Cavanaugh?"

"Yes?"

"Is your daughter okay?"

Cavanaugh considered the question for a moment and wondered how much the O'Reilly girl already knew.

"Well, yeah," said Cavanaugh. "I mean, I believe so. Why do you ask?"

"Well, she hasn't been to school in almost two weeks. Does she have the flu or something?"

Cavanaugh looked at the O'Reilly girl, then at Mrs. O'Reilly, then back at the O'Reilly girl.

He decided to go along with it.

"Um, yeah, that's what she's got—the flu," said Cavanaugh. "Or some kind of bug or something. It's been a really bad case. I'll tell her you asked for her."

The rain had shifted from a slow and steady drizzle to something less forgiving. Cavanaugh looked at Mrs. O'Reilly standing in the doorway and tried to imagine her gown getting wet, but it was hard for him to do that with her daughter right next to her cradling a Brett Kavanaugh bobblehead doll in her arms.

He scratched at something itchy inside his pants and tried to imagine regardless.

"Um, Cavanaugh?" said Mrs. O'Reilly. "Are you okay there?"

The question shook Cavanaugh out of his reverie. "Oh, um, of course. I mean, I, uh—well, good night, Missus O'Reilly," said Cavanaugh. "Let O'Reilly know I stopped by."

"Sure, Cavanaugh," said Mrs. O'Reilly. "Will do."

"Good night, Mister Cavanaugh," said the O'Reilly girl.

"Good night, O'Reilly girl," said Cavanaugh.

Mrs. O'Reilly coughed out a small cloud of smoke. "O'Reilly girl?" She remained at the doorway, bewildered, but Cavanaugh had already made it back to the sidewalk fast enough to pretend not to hear her, the wind now howling about his ears, the rain no longer gentle against his pockmarked face.

With one hand free and the other holding tightly onto his briefcase full of nothing, Cavanaugh was finally on his way home and there was no stopping him.

"Wind and rain be damned," said the voice.

"Wind and rain be damned," said Cavanaugh.

Cavanaugh Rings Two Doorbells

Something stopped Cavanaugh in front of his house.

He could see it peering through the upstairs window of the house across the street: a shadow. It was the same shadow that had watched him barf up the meat lasagna into the garbage bin, the same shadow that saw him hide what remained of his six-pack, the same shadow that had witnessed him abandon his daughter.

What was different this time, however, was that the shadow was already waiting for him at the window when he got there, as if it were expecting his return.

"Fuck you, shadow," said Cavanaugh, but the shadow did not move.

He said it louder: "Fuck you, shadow," but the shadow still would not budge.

He said it louder, then louder, but the shadow remained motionless. In fact, if anything, Cavanaugh observed, the shadow seemed to expand against the window, as if each successive curse word against it inflated its density.

Cavanaugh had had enough. He marched across the street, keeping his eye on the shadow as he marched. When he reached the front door of the shadow's house, he rang the doorbell. He waited for the sound of footsteps, the sound of a lock jiggling open, but heard nothing.

He rang the doorbell again.

Still, not a sound.

He rang it again and again in staccato-like succession.

Still, nothing.

Cavanaugh turned and stomped about the front lawn of the house, gazing up at the window as he stomped.

The shadow was still there, watching.

Cavanaugh stormed back to the front door, then banged away at it with both his fists.

No one from inside the house responded—not even the shadow's significant other, if it had one.

He kicked and banged, kicked and banged, rang the doorbell, rang it again, and then kicked and banged some more.

Still, no one came to the door, and not a sound came from within.

Cavanaugh walked onto the front lawn again, and looked up at the window.

The shadow was still there.

"Fine, have it your way, motherfucker," said Cavanaugh.

Cavanaugh lumbered across the street, back to the front of his own house. He looked back at the window across the street one more time.

The shadow was still there, unmoving, unbending and, still, watching.

Cavanaugh turned back to his own front door and rang the doorbell, but no one answered. He slipped his hand into his coat and felt around for his keys.

His pocket began to jingle.

MRS. O'REILLY TOSSES OUT THE GARBAGE

"MEN," MUTTERED Mrs. O'Reilly, as she held the bobblehead doll up to the one dim light that was still on in the kitchen. It was the very same doll that triggered her decision to tell her husband to hit the road or else. Just the thought of her daughter holding, let alone sleeping with, such a doll infuriated her all over again.

"Kavanaugh," she muttered.

She then thought of the man who had returned the doll to her daughter.

Cavanaugh.

Cavanaugh and Kavanaugh.

She shook her head. There was nothing at all funny about it to her.

She decided to call Mrs. Cavanaugh, a woman she had only spoken to two or three times on the phone, and whose car she had seen pass by her house twice daily. She had to tell her that what her husband presented to her daughter was not appropriate, and that the very man who was sleeping with her in her bed thought there was nothing wrong with giving a young girl a doll of a man whom she believed was a serial sexual predator.

She was about to pick up the phone when she saw a very large shadow moving along the kitchen window. Was it O'Reilly finally coming home, or was it just a car swishing its way down the road? Or was it Cavanaugh coming back to apologize? Perhaps, unlike O'Reilly, Cavanaugh had not known that the doll was in fact supposed to be Brett Kavanaugh, and having just realized his mistake, he just wanted to come back and say that, unlike her husband, he would have never in a million years had given such a doll to her daughter had he known the doll's true identity because he, too, believed the man behind the doll was a serial sexual predator.

The shadow on the window grew larger.

"Cavanaugh," whispered Mrs. O'Reilly under the lone dim light.

"Mom?"

Mrs. O'Reilly turned and screamed, dropping the bobblehead onto the floor. The loud crack made her jump, but she quickly caught her breath when she realized the shadow had just been her daughter's all along.

"Mom, who were you talking to?"

"Oh, it's you," said Mrs. O'Reilly. "No one, love. I was speaking to no one."

"I thought you said you were going to throw the Brett doll out."

"Oh, you bet I am. I am going to go right outside and toss it into the garbage bin right now. In the meantime, you hurry on upstairs and get yourself ready for bed. I'll meet you up there in a minute."

After her daughter ran up the stairs, Mrs. O'Reilly picked the doll up from the floor and carried it toward the front door. She had already put on her raincoat before having gotten lost in her thoughts about Cavanaugh and Kavanaugh.

She looked at the doll in her hands, its shattered face, and gritted her teeth.

"Kavanaugh," she muttered.

Outside, the rain came down hard. As she walked down the driveway toward the garbage bin, Mrs. O'Reilly could hear the swish and slosh of a car making its way up the road.

When the car had passed, and she had tossed the bobblehead into the bin, she turned and looked back at her house, and gazed up at one of the upstairs windows.

There, in the middle of the frame and behind the glass, a shadow appeared. It was shaped like a small head with two pigtails at either end.

Cavanaugh Reaches for His Beloved

No lights were on inside the Cavanaugh house. It was dark and quiet. The only sounds came from outside.

The hiss of the rain.

The howl of the wind.

A car sloshing down the road.

Cavanaugh had not been in his house in weeks, but he knew the terrain well, even in the dark. He considered for a moment turning on the lights in the foyer but decided against it, preferring to keep them off as long as he could, for he feared the prospect of alarming his wife and daughter over his undoubtedly altered appearance.

He called out his wife's name in the dark.

No answer.

He called out his daughter's name.

No answer.

He walked into the kitchen and emptied his pockets onto the counter: his keys, his wallet, his phone, the stolen phone charger.

He plugged the charger into an outlet below the counter, then plugged his phone into the charger. The charger lit up immediately, its neon-rainbow colors aglow in the dark.

Guess I hadn't lied to the waitress after all, pondered Cavanaugh.

He walked back out of the kitchen, went over to the staircase, and called up the stairs.

"Missus Cavanaugh."

No answer.

"Cavanaugh's daughter."

No answer.

Perhaps Cavanaugh's daughter is asleep, figured Cavanaugh, and perhaps Mrs. Cavanaugh is in the shower.

Cavanaugh walked quietly up the stairs, his coat still on his back, his briefcase full of nothing still in hand. He could not see the stairs, but his feet had good memory, having no trouble locating them in the dark.

When he reached the top of the stairs, the lights were all off there as well. He could see that both the door to his daughter's bedroom and the door to the master bedroom were wide-open.

He entered his daughter's bedroom. He knew she never slept with the door open, but he called out into the dark regardless.

"Cavanaugh's daughter."

No response.

The room smelled like bubblegum to Cavanaugh.

He flicked on the light.

Everything was put away. There was nothing on her desk and nothing on her chest of drawers. No books, no toys, no pens—not anything. Even her pin-up calendar was put away.

The only thing that was not put away was the Brett Kavanaugh bobblehead doll that O'Reilly had given her. It stood there on her nightstand next to her bed, its tiny bat in its tiny hands. There was nothing to distinguish it from the former one she had. The only difference was that instead of always watching over the bed as the former one had, this one was staring right at Cavanaugh, smirking.

Cavanaugh walked over to the nightstand and pressed the button.

The bobblehead came to life immediately, but seemed to have more energy in its movements than the one that had kept him company on his travels.

Perhaps it's just the batteries, figured Cavanaugh. He watched it bobble, then stop, its face still transfixed on his own.

His briefcase full of nothing still in hand, Cavanaugh turned around and headed back toward the doorway, flicked off the lights, and left the room.

He walked down the hallway a few steps and entered the master bedroom. With his daughter not in the house, he figured Mrs. Cavanaugh was not present either, but he surveyed the room just the same.

"Missus Cavanaugh?"

No response.

The room smelled like cleaning products to Cavanaugh, and felt unusually cold to him. Like the other rooms in the house, the lights were off.

In the dark, Cavanaugh walked to where he knew the master bathroom was. He reached out his hand and could tell the door was wide-open there as well.

He flicked on the light.

Mrs. Cavanaugh was not in the shower stall—or on the toilet bowl, for that matter. There was a shampoo bottle he did not recognize sitting on the shelf of the stall, but otherwise the stall looked the same as it had always looked.

His bar of soap was still lying in the corner, fermented and half-used.

Cavanaugh looked across from the shower stall and was startled to see someone in the mirror he did not recognize: himself.

He looked haggard, starved. His eyes were bloodshot, their corners full of crust. Despite the shag of his newly grown beard, the pock-marks on his cheeks seemed larger to him now, more indented. The hair on his head had grown longer as well, but his scalp seemed somehow more exposed—sunburnt perhaps, figured Cavanaugh, or maybe it was just eczema.

His lips looked charred, and there was a red irritation about his mouth. His ears were scabbing in the back, on the tips, on the insides, and along the edges, and he could see the marks on his skin where he had done his scratching.

He opened his mouth. His teeth were a blend of yellow and brown, with particles large and small stuck between them. His gums looked inflamed, even blistered in some parts.

His belly still protruded some, but it was less broad now, its pouch more ball-shaped. This new contour to his stomach made his breasts—or his "man-boobs," as his daughter once called them before being scolded by her mother—droop less like semi-deflated balloons as they once had and more like a pair of bruised melons that had gone spoiled.

Cavanaugh took off his coat, unzipped his pants, pulled down his boxers, and studied his privates in the mirror. His groin and scrotum looked rash-ridden, lacerated—their appearance alone made him itchy and sore all over.

Cavanaugh continued to look at his reflection in the mirror.

His reflection continued to look at him.

When he finished his looking, Cavanaugh took the rest of his clothes off and got in the shower. He tried to pull his bar of soap from the corner of the stall, but it remained stuck.

The water felt hot to Cavanaugh, but not so hot as to become prickly and disagreeable with the red scales covering his body. Water and steam were good for the sores, yet his crevices itched on regardless.

He considered masturbating in the shower, figuring it might offer some worthwhile relief and release, but the chafing about his privates posed an insurmountable distraction for him. He then tried to meditate in the thick of it all, but the voice inside his head kept talking to him.

"I'm hungry," said the voice.

"I'm thirsty," said the voice.

"I could use a drink," said the voice.

"Let's order in," said the voice.

Cavanaugh was about halfway through the longest shower he had ever taken when he put his face up against the translucent door of the stall and tried to see through it. He could just barely make it out, but there it was, standing upright on the tiled-floor of the steam-filled bathroom, waiting for him to come out: his briefcase full of nothing.

But Cavanaugh was not going to make his beloved briefcase wait any longer: he opened the stall door, reached his arm out about as far out as it could go, grabbed the briefcase full of nothing, and pulled it into the shower.

He held the briefcase by his side until the shower ended.

CAVANAUGH MAKES A CHANGE

CAVANAUGH WAS PLEASED to find his nighttime undershirts and boxers where he had always found them when he opened his dresser in the master bedroom. In fact, it appeared as though his stock of underwear in general had been replenished in the days and weeks since he had left the house, for there were pairs in the drawers he had never seen before.

After quickly putting on a pair of boxers with shamrocks on them along with a white undershirt, he grabbed his bathrobe that was still hanging in the bedroom closet, and headed toward the staircase.

The lights were still off when he got down the stairs. When he reached the den, he opened the door that went directly into the garage.

Cavanaugh flicked on the light. Mrs. Cavanaugh's car was nowhere to be found.

He flicked the lights back off, went back into the den, and walked around to the kitchen.

It was getting late, and Cavanaugh wondered where his wife and daughter could possibly be. Perhaps they had gone out for dinner—or better yet, dinner and a movie.

"Yeah, that must be it," said Cavanaugh aloud, in the pitch-black of his kitchen.

But it was a school night, wasn't it? Then again, the O'Reilly girl said his daughter had not been to school in almost two weeks.

Two weeks. That was a long time to be absent from school. Well, at least it wasn't three or four weeks, Cavanaugh figured. Besides, he had been gone even longer than that. Or had he? It all felt like a dream to him. He had slept and drank his way through most of it.

But he was still thirsty.

I could use a drink.

And so, too, was the voice.

He opened the refrigerator door, creating some light in the room. It was all juice and dairy, vegetables and fruits—stuff he had not the stomach for. Just the thought of drinking milk or eating a carrot made him nauseous.

Cavanaugh closed the door.

"But I'm starving," said the voice.

"Me, too," said Cavanaugh.

"Let's order in then," said the voice.

"Yes," said Cavanaugh. "Let's order in right now."

Cavanaugh pulled his phone from the charger and dialed his favorite restaurant for deliveries.

A voice answered on the second ring—a voice whose owner was the same young man that always answered such calls whenever Cavanaugh made them.

"This is Tommy's. How may I help you this evening?"

"I'd like to order a delivery."

"Let me guess: one well-done cheddar Tommyburger with a side order of garlic fries, and one can of Pepsi."

"How'd you know that?"

"You order the same thing every time. I recognized your phone number. And your voice. Though it's been a while, I guess. So, will that be all tonight?"

"Actually, that's not what I want to order this time."

The young man on the other end of the line feigned a gasp. "It's not?"

"Nope. Going to try something different."

"Go for it, sir. What would you like?"

"Got any buffalo wings on the menu?"

"Sure. How many?"

"I'll have the forty-for-forty."

"Pardon?"

"The forty wings for forty bucks. I'll have that."

"Um, sir, I don't believe we have something like that here."

"Well, how much would forty wings be then?"

"Forty wings?"

"No, make it fifty."

"Fifty?"

"Better yet, make it sixty."

"You want sixty wings?"

"Yup. Sixty. With the house sauce."

"Okay, so, just give me one second, sir, so I can jot that down for you here. You want sixty . . . with . . . the . . . house . . . sauce."

"Yup. How much will that be?"

"Well, we generally charge a buck-twenty-five a wing here, sir, but since you're ordering so many at once, and you've been such a loyal customer, I'm going to cap you out at sixty bucks."

"So sixty for sixty?"

"That's correct. Sixty for sixty, with the house sauce."

"And bleu cheese."

"And . . . bleu . . . cheese . . . So, sixty for sixty with the house sauce and bleu cheese—plus a can of Pepsi, right?"

"Nope, a can of Guinness."

"I'm so sorry, sir, but we're out of Guinness here, and we don't sell our beer in cans. We have bottles of Budweiser, Bud Light, Amstel Light, Sam Adams, Rolling—"

"Make it Sam Adams then."

"You got it. So, the sixty wings for sixty bucks with the house sauce and bleu cheese on the side, plus a bottle of Sam Ad—"

"No, a six-pack. A six-pack of Sam Adams."

"A six-pack of Sam Adams? You mean like six bottles?"

"Yup."

"Okay, six bottles then—now we're talking. So, let me go through your order here once more. Sixty wings for sixty bucks with the house sauce and bleu cheese on the side, plus six bottles of Sam Adams. Will that be all?"

"That is all."

"Okay, so, your total plus tax is going to be—"

"You can just charge it to my account. You have my credit card number on file, right?"

"Yup, we sure do. So, we'll have someone out to you in about forty-five, maybe fifty minutes."

"Forty-five, fifty minutes?"

"Well, you know, with the weather the way it is and all, and it *is* a lot of wings—there are only so many we can fit on the grill."

"Oh, right. That's a good point."

"But we'll try our best to get it to you quicker—you being a valued customer and all."

"Appreciate it."

"Sure, don't mention it. Well, you have a good day, Mister—what's your last name again?"

"Cavanaugh."

"Oh, yeah, right. Cavanaugh. Like Brett Kavanaugh."

Cavanaugh thought about correcting him on the spelling but decided not to bother. "Yeah, sure. Like him."

"See you soon, Mister Kavanaugh."

"Yup. See you soon."

Cavanaugh hung up the phone and laid it down on the counter. He stood there in the dark, scratching his privates through his bathrobe, when he realized he forgot something of great import.

He picked up his phone again and dialed.

"This is Tommy's. How can I help you this—Mister Kavanaugh? Is that you again?

"I almost forgot," said Cavanaugh. "Garlic fries."

CAVANAUGH AND THE TOMMY

IT TOOK ABOUT AN HOUR, but the food finally arrived. The young man who delivered his order wore a see-through hooded poncho—for it was still raining, though not as heavy—and a T-shirt that said TOMMY'S across the chest.

Cavanaugh peered over the shoulder of the young man and noticed that the car he had arrived in had the same phone number painted across its side that Cavanaugh had dialed earlier.

"Are you the same fella I spoke with about my order?" said Cavanaugh.

The young man pulled down his hood halfway. His hair was brown and curly.

Like onion rings, thought Cavanaugh.

"Excuse me?"

"The fella I spoke with about my order—was that you?"

"Oh, no, sir—that was probably Tommy."

"You mean, the fella who owns the restaurant—that Tommy?"

"No, sir—that would be his father who owns it. His name is Tommy as well."

"I see. So what's your name then?"

"Tommy."

"For real?"

"Yes, sir."

"Are you related to the other two Tommies?"

"No, sir. Just a coincidence, I guess."

"Wow. Three Tommies. That's something."

"Yeah, it sure is."

Cavanaugh reached into his pocket, then remembered he was in his bathrobe. "Oh, shoot. You know what, I'm out of cash, but I think I got some change upstairs if you're willing to wait."

"Well, I'm kind of running behind schedule as it is, sir, but—"

"Heck, you know what? Just tell Tommy—you know, the Tommy who took my order?—tell him that he can charge twenty-percent to my credit card. He's got it on file there, but if there's a problem, tell him to give me a ring—he knows my number. Just tell him Cavanaugh, and he'll know."

"Cavanaugh. You mean, like Brett Kavanaugh?"

Cavanaugh looked at the Tommy.

The Tommy looked at Cavanaugh.

Cavanaugh moved his shoulders up, then down.

"Yeah, I suppose," said Cavanaugh. "Like him. Like Brett Kavanaugh."

"Well, that'll be real easy to remember then."

"Yeah, I'm sure it will be." Cavanaugh turned and was about to shut the door, but he did not shut it quickly enough.

"Hey, you're not him, are ya?"

Cavanaugh turned back to face the Tommy standing in front of his doorway. "What's that?"

"I said you're not him, are ya? Brett Kavanaugh, I mean. You're not Brett Kavanaugh, are ya, Mister Kavanaugh?

"I don't know, you tell me," said Cavanaugh. "Do I look like Brett Kavanaugh to you?"

The Tommy squinted as he assessed Cavanaugh's appearance, tilting his head left and right as he inspected.

"Hmm," said the Tommy, "it's kind of hard to tell. The last time I saw Brett Kavanaugh, he was wearing a cap on his head."

"A cap?"

"Yeah, a cap. A baseball cap. Saw a clip of him on TV—on the late news, I think. When he delivered the opening pitch at that ballgame and . . ."

"Oh, right, right—the opening pitch, right."

". . . threw that perfect slider."

"Yeah, yeah—I saw that, too. I was at the game."

"You were?"

"Yup."

"So. . .?"

"So . . . what?"

"So, was it you who threw that slider then?"

"Me? No, no, no. Nah, I was in the stands."

"In the stands?"

"Yup. In the stands. Watching the game with my little daughter."

"Wait—you have a daughter?"

"Um, yeah, but—"

"Hmm . . . let's see here," said the Tommy. "You have a daughter . . . You have a daughter just like Brett Kavanaugh has a daughter . . . Um . . . Mister Kavanaugh . . . are you sure you're not Brett Kavanaugh?"

"I'm quite sure. Besides, I think he has two daughters, actually."

"Do you have two daughters, Mister Kavanaugh?"

"Nope, I have one."

"Are you sure you just have one?"

"Yup. I'm sure."

"So, are you, like, maybe related to him though? Like, maybe you're his brother or cousin or something?"

Cavanaugh stared deep into the Tommy's eyes and saw wonder.

The Tommy stared deep into Cavanaugh's eyes and saw a Kavanaugh.

"Nope. Not related," said Cavanaugh. "Not brothers. Not cousins. Not anything. Not in the slightest."

"You're sure now, right?"

"Yeah, I'm quite sure of it. In fact—"

"In fact . . .?"

Cavanaugh looked into the Tommy's eyes again. He was a hopeful Tommy, he could tell, and to reveal the correct spelling of his surname now would only serve to dampen the young man's spirits.

"You're right, Mister Kavanaugh," said the Tommy. "I am a hopeful Tommy."

"Wait a second," said Cavanaugh. "You just heard me say that?"

"Say what?"

"You heard me say that you are a hopeful Tommy?"

"Well, yeah, Mister Kavanaugh. You just said it inches from my face, dude. Though I have to say it was sort of weird because you said it like it was in the past and as if I wasn't right here in front of you. You said, 'He was a hopeful Tommy' rather than 'You are a hopeful Tommy,' which, like I said, you're totally right about—I mean, a lot of people say I'm a glass-is-half-full kind of guy, so it's not like it's something I haven't heard before."

Cavanaugh leaned in closer to the Tommy. "So, you can hear the voice then too, right?"

"The voice?"

"The voice that said that you were hopeful."

"Well, yeah—of course I heard it. I mean, it's your voice, ain't it? Like I said, I'm standing right in front of you—how can I not hear it?"

Cavanaugh looked at the Tommy.

The Tommy looked at Cavanaugh.

"Yup," said the Tommy. "I did look at you. In fact, I'm still looking at you."

"Dear god," said Cavanaugh.

"Dear god what?" said the Tommy.

"The voice."

"The voice?"

"Listen, I gotta go. Been nice chatting with you."

"Yeah, same here, Mister Kavanaugh. I'll let Tommy Junior know about the twenty-percent."

"Yup, twenty-percent. You got it."

"Alright, Mister Cavanaugh. Thanks so much. You have a good—"
Cavanaugh shut the door.

He was about to head to the kitchen with his dinner delivery, but something made him turn back toward the door.

He peered through the peephole. The Tommy was still standing there, his back to the front of the door, holding a phone to his ear inside the hood of his poncho.

"Yeah, Tommy? This is Tommy. Yeah, I'm quite sure it's him, though he kind of talks kind of funny. Also, it looks like he's grow-ing a beard or something. But it's him alright. It's Brett Kavanaugh. You owe me twenty bucks, dude."

CAVANAUGH IS A DOG

CAVANAUGH NODDED his head at the bus driver.

The bus driver nodded his head at the busboy.

The busboy nodded his head at the waiter.

The waiter nodded his head at the waitress.

The waitress nodded her head at the officer.

The officer nodded his head at the bobblehead.

The bobblehead nodded its head at Cavanaugh's daughter.

Cavanaugh's daughter nodded her head at Mrs. Cavanaugh.

Mrs. Cavanaugh nodded her head at Mrs. O'Reilly.

Mrs. O'Reilly nodded her head at O'Reilly.

O'Reilly nodded his head at the O'Reilly girl.

The O'Reilly girl nodded her head at the Tomboy Twins.

The Tomboy Twins nodded their heads at the Tommy.

The Tommy nodded his head at the other Tommy.

The other Tommy nodded his head at the man who might be Brett Kavanaugh.

The man who might be Brett Kavanaugh nodded his head at the shadow in the window.

The shadow in the window nodded its head at the shadow on top of Missus Cavanaugh.

The shadow on top of Missus Cavanaugh nodded its head at Missus Cavanaugh.

Missus Cavanaugh nodded her head at the young boy inside Cavanaugh's head.

The young boy inside Cavanaugh's head nodded his head at the dog up the road.

The dog up the road nodded its head at the dog down the road.

The dog down the road nodded its head at Cavanaugh.

Somewhere down the road, Cavanaugh barked.

Cavanaugh Misses His Bed

"First, you drank one bottle of Sam Adams," said the voice.

"Then I had another right after," said Cavanaugh.

"Yup. Then you had about a dozen wings in a row," said the voice. "Sometimes you dipped them in the house sauce, but sometimes you did not dip them at all."

"That sounds about right," said Cavanaugh. "And then I had another bottle of Sam Adams."

"Right," said the voice. "Even though you have mixed feelings about the taste of Sam Adams, that is indeed what you did: you had another bottle."

"Yup," said Cavanaugh. "And then I had about fourteen or fifteen more wings, I believe."

"Nah, it was more like eighteen or nineteen more—without even taking a single sip of Sam Adams in between."

"Pretty impressive, eh?"

"Yes, pretty impressive, indeed," said the voice. "But you weren't quite through yet, were you?"

"Nope," said Cavanaugh. "Not even close to through. In fact, I started working through the fourth bottle of Sam Adams right about then."

"Yes, you started on it, but you did not quite finish it right away," said the voice.

"That's because of the garlic fries," said Cavanaugh.

"Yes, the garlic fries," said the voice. Those were quite tasty—were they not?"

"Oh, they *were* quite tasty," said Cavanaugh, licking his lips. "Quite tasty, indeed."

"If I recall correctly, you had eaten through about half of them," said the voice.

"Um, yeah—that sounds about right, more or less."

"But then . . ."

"But then?"

"But then you felt something in your stomach—did you not?"

"Yup, I felt something in my stomach. Right in the lower region there."

"Just a little something, right?" said the voice.

"Yeah, just a little something," said Cavanaugh. "Nothing out of the ordinary. Just a little something."

"But there was no need for concern, was there?" said the voice.

"Nah, no need—no need at all," said Cavanaugh. "I figured if I just drank what remained of the fourth bottle of Sam Adams, that little something—well, it would go away on its own."

"And did it?" said the voice.

"It sure did," said Cavanaugh.

"And then you had about ten more wings," said the voice.

"Right," said Cavanaugh. "Though I decided to lay off of the house sauce while I ate those ten wings in order to make sure that my stomach settled down a bit first."

"Yes, I remember your making that decision," said the voice. "And that decision, Mister Cavanaugh, was a wise decision—a very wise decision, indeed. Especially considering—if you don't mind me saying—that, by then, you were drunk off your ass."

"Well, yeah—I suppose that is fair to say," said Cavanaugh. "In that crucial moment of decision-making, I was indeed just that: drunk off my ass."

"And that decision," said the voice, "was a decision that allowed you the freedom to plow through the twenty or so remaining wings."

"That's correct," said Cavanaugh. "And that's when I remembered that I still had the bleu cheese dip, whose container I hadn't yet even opened."

"And the bleu cheese was more agreeable, was it not?"

"Agreeable?"

"To your stomach. Was it not more agreeable to your stomach than the house sauce was?"

"Oh, yes—way more agreeable," said Cavanaugh. "Way, way more. I mean, having that fifth bottle of Sam Adams probably helped as well."

"Yes, it did help," said the voice. "In washing it down, certainly."

"And creating more room," said Cavanaugh.

"More room?" said the voice.

"For eating the remainder of the garlic fries, I mean," said Cavanaugh. "It created more room in my stomach for that—remember?"

"Remember?" said the voice. "How could I *not* remember? After all, that's when the flatulence began."

"Flatulence? By flatulence, you mean farting, right?"

"Precisely," said the voice. "Farting."

"Oh, right—the farting," said Cavanaugh. "Well, that was some pretty nasty farting, was it not?"

"Oh, pretty nasty indeed, Mister Cavanaugh," said the voice. "Very, very nasty. And then when you finished up all the garlic fries, do you remember what happened next?"

"Hmm," said Cavanaugh. "I'm not sure if I quite remember that part, but let me guess."

"I'm all ears, Mister Cavanaugh," said the voice. "Go ahead and guess."

"Okay, here goes my guess," said Cavanaugh. "My guess is that I started on the sixth bottle of Sam Adams."

"Well, you definitely did start the sixth bottle of Sam Adams—and finished it," said the voice. "But that was not the part to which I was referring."

"It wasn't?" said Cavanaugh.

"I'm afraid not," said the voice. "No, what I was referring to was the licking."

"The licking?"

"The licking of the house sauce."

"I licked the house sauce?"

"All of it."

"All of it?"

"Every last remaining drop that was left in that container. You licked it and sucked it dry."

"Good god," said Cavanaugh.

"Good god, indeed," said the voice. "Which was why you began to feel a little something again."

"A little something?"

"In your stomach. That little something in the lower region of your stomach—it had returned."

"It had?"

"It most certainly had. And that's when the rumbling started."

"Rumbling? What rumbling?"

"In the lower region of your stomach, Mister Cavanaugh—there was a rumbling in the lower region of your stomach that had begun right after you finished licking and sucking the rest of the house sauce out of its container. Ring a bell?"

"You know," said Cavanaugh, "now that you mention it, I think it does ring a bell."

"Of course it rings a bell, you drunken nitwit. How can it not ring a bell? In fact, the lower region of your stomach is still rumbling at this very moment."

"Yeah, I can sort of feel it right now, actually," said Cavanaugh. "The rumbling, I mean. Feels kind of funny. Makes me want to shit and laugh at the same time."

"And your boxers," said the voice.

"My boxers?" said Cavanaugh. "What about my boxers?"

"Well, you can smell it, can't you?" said the voice. "Can't you smell what's inside them?"

"Smell what?" said Cavanaugh. "What's inside them? I don't smell a damn thing."

"Smell, Cavanaugh," said the voice. "Open up your big, fat nostrils and smell. Take a fucking goddamn whiff and smell, for christ sake."

"Dear god," said Cavanaugh.

"Dear god, indeed," said the voice.

"When did this happen?" said Cavanaugh.

"I told you already," said the voice. "It happened shortly after you licked and sucked the remaining house sauce out of its container. And then you went upstairs to change into a clean pair of boxers, but by the time you got upstairs, you forgot all about changing."

"Upstairs? I went upstairs?"

"You're upstairs right now, you buffoon."

"I am?"

"You are."

"But then why don't I recollect coming up the—"

"Because you blacked out again. You blacked out, and now you are upstairs."

"Where am I upstairs?"

"In the master bedroom," said the voice. "On the floor."

"On the floor?"

"Next to the bed."

"But why am I on the floor, next to the bed? Why am I not *on* the bed instead?"

"Because you missed, Cavanaugh! You missed!"

"I missed?"

"The bed," said the voice. "You missed it. You flopped yourself backward, aiming to land on the bed, but you missed."

"And now I'm here on the floor."

"And now you're there on the floor."

"In the dark."

"In the dark."

"With my back aching."

"With your back aching."

"And my boxers all smelly and wet."

"And your boxers all smelly and wet."

"Wow. Well, I could use a drink."

"Well, I suppose I, too, could use a drink."

"But I can't get myself off the floor."

"You *must* get yourself off the floor."

"I *must*?"

"They're coming, Cavanaugh."

"Who's coming?"

"Your wife. Your daughter. And—"

"And?"

"Never mind that now. Just get up, Cavanaugh. Get up off the floor and run."

"Run?"

"Away. Get up off the floor right now and run away."

"Run away? To where?"

"Anywhere. Anywhere but inside this house."

"But I can't."

"You must."

"I won't."

"You will."

"Good night."

"Good night?"

"Sleep tight."

"Sleep tight?"

"Don't let the bedbugs—"

Cavanaugh yawned, then drifted into unconsciousness. Somewhere in his dreams, a dog barked.

CAVANAUGH IN THE DARK

He was still in the midst of a dream when he heard the sound of the station wagon entering the garage. It was not until he heard the jingling sound of his wife's car keys that he was fully awake.

He could hear someone whispering at the foot of the staircase: "She needs to be carried up to her room."

It was Mrs. Cavanaugh doing the whispering, Cavanaugh knew, but it surprised him—and even sparked a momentary feeling of delight and solidarity—hearing her speak to herself in the third person.

"Be careful with her," said Mrs. Cavanaugh. "Don't wake her up."

He imagined Mrs. Cavanaugh carrying Cavanaugh's daughter up the stairs, the little girl's face against her shoulder, an angel's breath against her neck.

But Cavanaugh wondered: Could Mrs. Cavanaugh still manage such a task? Their little daughter was not so little anymore. Based on the echo of her footsteps against the staircase, it sounded to Cavanaugh as though Mrs. Cavanaugh was limping under the weight and could use a hand.

Cavanaugh considered for a moment getting up from the floor and helping Mrs. Cavanaugh carry their daughter to her bed, but there were more reasons to lie low for a bit and not help. For one, he did not want to startle her. The thought of Mrs. Cavanaugh screaming in the dark and losing her balance on the stairs, their precious daughter in her arms, was too much for Cavanaugh to bear.

Then there was the fact that he was still drunk—more to the point: he was not completely certain that what he was hearing was real or just some alcohol-induced hallucination.

There was also a warm, semi-moist, cakey feeling in his boxers, surely the end-product of hastily-consumed buffalo wings, garlic fries, bleu cheese, and whatever in the world was in that house sauce he had licked and sucked out from its container.

Further complicating his desire to assist was the pulsating pain running up and down his back for having landed on it when he had entirely missed the bed, for how would he even be able to carry his daughter up the remaining stairs and into her bedroom with such an injury?

Needless to say, it was an easy decision for Cavanaugh: he would forego assisting Mrs. Cavanaugh and would instead remain where he lay until the right opportunity presented itself.

"Easy does it," whispered Mrs. Cavanaugh. The clarity of her whisper suggested to Cavanaugh that she was now closer to the upstairs hallway. "I'll meet you in the bedroom."

Perhaps Mrs. Cavanaugh has a voice inside her own head keeping her company just like I have one, figured Cavanaugh. They were two kindred spirits after all.

Cavanaugh felt as close to Mrs. Cavanaugh as ever before.

He remained in silence on the floor of the far side of the bed, as he listened to the sound of footsteps on the hardwood coming from the side closest to the doorway.

It was surely Mrs. Cavanaugh, the sweet fragrance of her perfume unmistakable. He could hear the creak and swish of the bed as she collapsed backward on top of it, her high-heeled shoes dropping to the floor with two small thuds, one after the other. He listened with complete stillness in the dark as she fussed about the pillows. She was breathing heavily—not surprising to Cavanaugh given the energy she must have exerted to carry their daughter up all those stairs.

It was still not a good time to present himself, concluded Cavanaugh—not with the condition he was in.

He looked about the foot of the nightstand next to him. He could barely make it out, but he could see the edge of his beloved briefcase jutting out from between the nightstand and the wall next to it, where he always had kept it on nights before work. It smelled very clean to him from where he lay—much cleaner than *he* must have smelled, for sure.

Cavanaugh heard a closing of a door from somewhere beyond the master bedroom—out in the hallway, most likely.

Must be Cavanaugh's daughter shutting the door to her bedroom, figured Cavanaugh. Or perhaps it was the sound of her closing her closet door, having retrieved her pajamas for the night.

From wherever his wife and daughter had come, Cavanaugh knew it was very late in the evening—too late for a child to be out of the house on a school night, regardless if she was attending class or staying home the next day. But who was he to criticize, a husband and father having abandoned his—

He heard footsteps coming from the hallway beyond the master bedroom.

Must be Cavanaugh's daughter heading into our bedroom, surmised Cavanaugh—perhaps she had been sleeping with Mrs. Cavanaugh since her father's absence.

But the footsteps were uneven and heavy against the wood of the floor, and sounded more like the audible output of boots to him than the bare feet of a small child.

"I'm in here," whispered Mrs. Cavanaugh.

The footsteps came to a stop. There was a heavy breathing that was no longer her own.

Who was she talking to now? Her daughter? Herself?

Cavanaugh remained still and listened. He looked up toward the window. He heard the sound of a car swishing down the wet road, its headlights forming a momentary spotlight in the bedroom as it passed by in the night.

"I'm right here on the bed," whispered Mrs. Cavanaugh.

"I can't see nothing," whispered a voice back. "It's too fucking dark in here."

Cavanaugh knew immediately the voice was not the voice of Mrs. Cavanaugh, nor was it a voice coming from inside her head. And it certainly was not the voice of Cavanaugh's daughter either.

It was the voice of a man.

It was the voice of O'Reilly.

Cavanaugh clenched his fists and gritted his teeth as the temperature and very chemistry of his body went into flux.

Still, he remained silent and listened.

Why should I give O'Reilly the satisfaction? reasoned Cavanaugh. Especially given the pathetic condition I'm in.

O'Reilly.

Cavanaugh listened to the familiar rhythm of his neighbor's limp against the hardwood, and a sudden wave of thought swept over him: The limp? What limp? It was probably not even a real limp, just a ploy to gain sympathy from others.

A fool's ploy, thought Cavanaugh. But a ploy that seemed to be working well against his wife, he admitted.

"Shut the door behind you," whispered Mrs. Cavanaugh. "Walk toward my voice and you'll find the bed."

The door to the bedroom banged shut.

"Damn it, O'Reilly," said Mrs. Cavanaugh. "You're gonna wake my little angel up."

"Oops. Sorry, Missus Cavanaugh," whispered O'Reilly back. "It was an accident. Can't see a damn thing in here."

"Follow my voice."

"I'm following, I'm following."

Something bumped against the bed, nudged it across the floor a bit.

"Found it now?" whispered Mrs. Cavanaugh. "I'm right in the middle of it."

"Okay, I got ya now."

"Take your boots off first. I don't want you tracking any filth onto the bed."

"Yes, ma'am."

"Here, let me help you with that."

Cavanaugh could hear the jingle.

Belt against buckle.

Then two large thuds against the floor, one after the other.

Boot against wood.

"Touch me right there," said Mrs. Cavanaugh.

"Where?" said O'Reilly. "Right there?"

"No," said Mrs. Cavanaugh. "Give me your hand. Right there."

"Oh, I got it now," said O'Reilly.

"Be gentle with me," said Mrs. Cavanaugh. "Be gentle."

"However you like it, Missus Cavanaugh. That's what it'll be."

"Oh, Cavanaugh," said Mrs. Cavanaugh. "Oh, god, Cavanaugh. Cavanaugh. Cavanaugh."

"Oh, Missus Cavanaugh," said O'Reilly. "I love it when you call me Cavanaugh."

"Don't talk," said Mrs. Cavanaugh. "Please, whatever you do, don't talk."

Cavanaugh continued to remain silent as he listened to the wetness of their mouths against one another, the bed creaking softly beneath them. He could hear everything, and almost even feel it.

A jingling.

An unzipping.

An unfastening.

Fabrics falling swiftly to the ground. Something satin—Mrs. Cavanaugh's blouse—hit Cavanaugh—the *real* Cavanaugh—in the face. Cavanaugh squeezed the blouse in his hands, held it under his nose, but did not make a sound.

A thrusting.

A squeaking.

A sighing.

A moaning.

"Oh, Cavanaugh."

"Yes, Missus Cavanaugh."

"Oh, Cavanaugh, Cavanaugh."

"Yes, Missus Cavanaugh, yes, yes, yes."

It was all happening too fast for Cavanaugh. He mouthed the words to himself: *Help me.*

"I will help you," said the voice.

"Please," mouthed Cavanaugh. "Please make it go away."

"I will make it go away," said the voice.

Someone whispered: "Shh."

Another vehicle came swishing down the road, the twin beams of its headlights darting across the dark ceiling of the room.

A car.

A bus.

Another car.

A truck.

A bottlecap snapping open.

A bottleneck fizzing with foam.

A voice whispering inside a birthmarked head.

A dog barking somewhere down the road.

And Cavanaugh was asleep again.

Cavanaugh Reunites with His Beloved

Cavanaugh woke up to the sound of heavy snoring. It was still dark in the room, but in that darkness, he could feel something oozing from the insides of his mouth. He panicked for a moment, thinking that perhaps he had had a seizure of sorts while he had slept, but then something occurred to him, which, until he had come home and inspected himself in the bathroom mirror, had escaped his thinking: his teeth and gums had not been cleaned in weeks.

Like a dog unkempt, thought Cavanaugh. A bedraggled creature of the night. I belong in a hole, or somewhere underground, where things slither and crawl.

But for now, he was on the floor, lying with the dust mites, silent, still, waiting for movement from something other than himself, holding Mrs. Cavanaugh's satin blouse next to his cheek for security.

But no movement came. Not even from the bed next to and above him was there any movement—the bed that had been his own bed but was no longer. It now belonged to something that was outside of him, an artifact from his past passed on to others. He had now become a ghost—a ghost unworthy of haunting even the very floorboards that he himself had coasted about and creaked on for years.

His mouth ached and burned. He tried turning his face to the side, to see if that would take some of the weight off the pain, but the pain merely shifted as he turned. Whatever had been oozing inside his mouth began to trickle onto the floor.

His face now sideways, Cavanaugh turned his gaze to his briefcase full of nothing, which stood still and upright on the sliver of floor between nightstand and wall.

He reached his hand out toward the briefcase, his fingers caressing its vinyl edges. It was the only thing left in the room that was still his.

Seeing that the briefcase was beyond the reach of a firm grip from where he lay, Cavanaugh pulled his hand back toward himself, and scratched his groin in the dark: it was still itchy down there, but at least he could now feel parts of his body that he was not able to feel just hours earlier.

The other hand still clutched Mrs. Cavanaugh's satin blouse.

His back pain had mostly subsided, but, in addition to the burning ooze inside his mouth, there was a throbbing about the circumference of his head.

"I could use a drink," said the voice.

"No, no," said Cavanaugh. "Please don't say that now. Please don't say that."

"I could use a drink."

"Shut up, shut up, shut up."

The snoring broke abruptly, then continued. Cavanaugh had already decided on making it out of the bedroom without confrontation or, for that matter, even making his presence known. It was close to pitch-black in there, but unlike the other gentleman in the room, Cavanaugh was familiar enough with its landscape to know where everything was, his semi-inebriated state notwithstanding.

He listened to the rustling of the tree branches outside the window, and heard the piercing wail of a distant siren. He watched the ceiling and the far wall light up as the sound of another vehicle roared down the road. And then he slowly shifted his body away from the side of the bed, propping himself up on one elbow. He waited for another car on the road to zoom by before turning his body on all fours, masking whatever creaking he might make on the floorboards beneath him with the whir of air and engine.

The snoring carried on unabated and grew louder.

He wondered, for a moment, how Mrs. Cavanaugh could sleep through O'Reilly's heavy snoring, but then remembered that he was an occasional snorer as well—or so he was told.

Not this night though, luckily. Or, had he, in fact, snored, and they just had not been able to hear him in the heat of passion?

Perhaps he really was a ghost after all.

He knelt on one knee with his body upright, waiting for another car to pass. He waited for several minutes, but no sounds of a vehicle came, only the sounds of trees rustling, and—he can now hear it, though just barely, now that he was halfway off the floor—the faintest of jingling sounds.

A wind chime, perhaps, blowing in the wind, he figured.

Cavanaugh was about to postpone his mission and lower his body back down to the floor, when, suddenly, another vehicle came swishing down the road, beaming a light against the wall just over his shoulder.

He pushed off hard against the hardwood floor, generating a loud creak beneath him, but the roar of the vehicle—it sounded loud enough to Cavanaugh to be a truck—overrode any sound his own movement produced.

He was now standing, Mrs. Cavanaugh's blouse in one hand, the other hand reaching out, feeling its way through the dark. He could not see the bed, nor its occupants, but he recognized the soft, elegant rhythms of Mrs. Cavanaugh's breathing coming from very close by, and knew she was the one nearest to where he stood.

Another car passed by, and he took one step as it hummed along the road.

Shortly after, another car whizzed by, and he took a second step.

Something as small as a pebble rolled down from the inside of his boxers, off the back of his thigh, and out. He looked down and saw nothing on the floor beneath him.

Cavanaugh pivoted to his left, knowing his briefcase was within reach. He bent his body forward and felt the side of his head graze against what he knew had to be the lampshade. The lamp jostled a bit, but the breathing and snoring went on undisturbed.

Cavanaugh lowered himself further, reaching his hand out until it touched something that was hard and smooth and, from the way it buckled ever so gently, was light, and he knew then that his fingers had found what they had been looking for: his briefcase full of nothing.

He slid his fingers until they found the leathery texture of the handle, but something made him stop him in his tracks: it was a glistening dot, a tiny speck of light suspended in the dark. He reached down to touch it, then realized that the glistening speck was on his finger.

It was his wedding ring.

Cavanaugh caressed the ring with the fingers on his other hand, as if the very ring itself could feel his affection, but then his fingers locked and shook, and in almost a single swift motion, he clutched down hard on the ring and pulled it off his ring finger, before slamming it onto the invisible surface of the nightstand below.

The wedding ring rattled against the table.

Something on the bed jostled—something large.

The snoring and breathing came to an end.

"Whoa. What was that?" It was O'Reilly. "Who's out there? Cavanaugh, is that you?"

"What is it, O'Reilly?" said Mrs. Cavanaugh, half-unconscious. "What's going on?"

"I thought I heard something," said O'Reilly. "It must've just been a bad dream."

"There's nothing to be heard in here," said Mrs. Cavanaugh. "Just the trees and cars outside. Go back to sleep."

Cavanaugh could hear the sheets moving about, but knew that neither O'Reilly nor Mrs. Cavanaugh would see him through the thick dark of the room.

The heavy breathing and snoring started up again almost instantly, but Cavanaugh waited for several vehicles to go by before placing Mrs. Cavanaugh's blouse inside his briefcase. It took a few passing vehicles more before he deftly repeated the same tactic of blending in with the nighttime rustle-and-roar in order to creep around the foot of the king-size bed and make it to the other side of the room.

With every step, something rolled off the back of his leg from the inside of his boxers. He imagined O'Reilly and Mrs. Cavanaugh waking up in the morning to a trail of pebbles shaped like brown shamrocks scattered about the floorboards, forming a semicircle around the bed.

When Cavanaugh reached the doorway, another beam of light
from another passing vehicle reflected and rolled down the ceiling
and wall of the room, and, for a moment or two, Cavanaugh could
see O'Reilly's face flash before him, his wide snoring nose and open
mouth exposed in the light, the back of his head lying on the very
pillow that had been Cavanaugh's own for so many years. When the
light retreated, Cavanaugh could still hear the snoring—it was coming from both sides of the bed, like a duet of dueling tuba-blowers. He
briefly considered raising his briefcase over his head and smashing it
squarely on top of O'Reilly's face in the dark, the blood spattering all
over Mrs. Cavanaugh and the cream-colored comforter that had kept
she and Cavanaugh so warm and cozy over the years, but he quickly
cast such a vengeful thought aside.

*You can't protect me from him anyway. You're just a boy. And you
can't stay here now anyhow. You have a bus to catch.*

Cavanaugh quietly opened the door, then gently closed it, before
tiptoeing out to the safety of the narrow hallway, where he found himself in the dark again but now alone, save for his briefcase full of satin.

Cavanaugh Sees an Angel

Cavanaugh was about to take his first step down the stairs, when, suddenly, something made him pull his foot back.

He turned and looked at the closed doorway to his daughter's bedroom. It had been weeks since he had either seen or spoken to his daughter, let alone held her in his arms.

He stepped back onto the upstairs landing, and tiptoed up to his daughter's bedroom door.

Cavanaugh knew that Cavanaugh's daughter was a deep sleeper. He was more concerned about waking up the two adulterers in the master bedroom than waking up the child.

He turned the door gently with nary a creak, and entered his daughter's bedroom. He left the door open behind him so he would only have to put in half the work on the way out. A streetlamp outside her bedroom window provided just enough light for Cavanaugh to navigate the room and see its contents.

She was breathing softly in her sleep in the small bed in the far corner of the room, her freckled cheeks and strawberry hair sticking out from under the comforter, her serene face facing upward toward the ceiling. She was tucked under the covers—courtesy, Cavanaugh figured, of O'Reilly's handiwork—but Cavanaugh was relieved to see that she had not been changed into her pajamas by the sinner who had put her to bed.

On his daughter's nightstand stood the Brett Kavanaugh bobble-head doll, its little baseball cap glistening in the dark, its smirk just visible enough for Cavanaugh to delineate.

Cavanaugh wheeled his daughter's swivel desk chair up close to the bed, just a few feet or so away from it. Just as his rear-end made contact with the chair, he remembered the situation inside his boxers, but from the feel of them now, it seemed that the boxers were now completely free of what had been deposited and mashed about inside them.

Cavanaugh sat comfortably in the little swivel chair, watching and listening to his daughter as she breathed preciously in her sleep.

This alone, he thought, made the return home worth it.

In the quiet dark, he considered, on and off, waking her, or very carefully lifting her from the bed and carrying her out the door in his arms. Surely Mrs. Cavanaugh—or O'Reilly—must have left the car keys downstairs somewhere, thought Cavanaugh: he could place her in the backseat of the car, open the garage, and drive off with her for the day, or the week, or however long either of them wished. It was probably still another couple of hours before there would be any meaningful traffic on the road, so he would not have to worry as much about getting into an accident.

Or, better yet, he could carry her to the bus stop, and they could spend the day exploring the outskirts of the town. He could show her that plaza with the fountain he had discovered on that first morning he skipped work. He could take her to Corrigan's, share a bucket of wings, and show her off to the waitress there. Or maybe he could just take her out for lemonade and ice cream—perhaps that would even make her more amenable to going back to school. He would tell her that this phase he was going through—of coming and going and wandering about—well, it was just that—a phase—and he would tell her that soon he would be back in her life for good, and that everything will be back to normal with the three of them all together again—she, he and Mrs. Cavanaugh—and that what was going on now would just be a tiny blip before the long bright future ahead of her, and that this whole episode will be all but forgotten by the time she went off to some great college somewhere, far away from the reaches of any familial drama.

Cavanaugh looked down at his hands, studied his now ringless ring finger.

No, it would not be forgotten, he knew. There was no turning back the clock on this. Whether or not he sobered up soon, these days, these weeks in which he abandoned his home, his wife, his child—they would not be forgotten.

No, this will not be a blip.

It will be a stain.

An albatross.

A source of long-term damage to his daughter's psyche.

It would be the moment that forever altered the trajectory of her life for the worse.

Trauma had been inflicted upon her, and he, and no one else but he, was the inflictor.

"Your head," said the voice.

"What about my head?" whispered Cavanaugh.

"It's twitching," said the voice. "Wouldn't want your little angel to see that again now, would we?"

Cavanaugh placed a hand to his head and felt it twitch in the dark. He then pulled his hand away and gazed over at the bobblehead doll.

It was staring at him.

Smirking at him.

Mocking him.

Cavanaugh had had enough.

He leapt up from the desk chair, grabbed the bobblehead, and raised it over his head, casting a menacing shadow on the wall next to the bed.

Cavanaugh caught a glimpse of the shadow from the corner of his eye, saw his daughter's face—still calm and precious above the covers—and collapsed back into the swivel chair, the bobblehead dropping onto his lap.

It was all too much for Cavanaugh to bear. He watched over the sleeping child for a few minutes more, then closed his teary eyes, a doll cradled in his arms, a briefcase full of satin at his feet, drifting into a slumber he wished to never awaken from, in a room he wished to never leave.

CAVANAUGH THROWS A SLIDER

IN THE MIDST of another dream, he felt a warm hand touch his face—a small hand.

"Daddy."

Half-awake now, he felt it again.

"Daddy."

A third time, on his arm.

"Daddy."

He opened his eyes and saw his freckle-faced, red-haired angel leaning back against the edge of her twin bed. Next to her, on the nightstand, was the bobblehead doll, watching over them.

She must have removed it from my lap and placed it back where it had been, figured Cavanaugh.

He prayed that was the case.

"Daddy?"

He gazed back at his daughter and smiled. "Angel," he whispered.

"Daddy," she whispered back. She threw herself at him and hugged him tight around his neck.

"It's good to see you, angel."

"It's good to see you, Daddy."

She giggled.

"Hey, what's so funny?"

"Your beard. That's what's funny."

"Oh, you think my beard is funny, do you?"

"Uh-huh."

"Do you like it?"

She grinned and bit her lip, then shrugged her shoulders. "You look like a pirate."

"A pirate? Arr."

"And you *smell* like a pirate, too."

"Oh, I do, do I? Arrrr."

He pulled her into his arms.

She giggled again.

"Daddy?"

"Yes, angel?"

"Are you going to stay home now?"

Cavanaugh looked into his daughter's eyes, and then down at his lap. "Soon, angel. Maybe soon."

She bit her lip again, the grin evaporating from her face. "So, if you're not going to stay home now, why'd you come back?"

"To see you, angel. That's why I came. To see how you were doing. Are you doing okay?"

She lowered her face, then leaned into him, her head shuddering against his shoulder as she wept into his chest.

Cavanaugh felt the urge to weep with her, but held himself back.

"Oh, it's okay, angel. It's okay. Things will be okay soon. I just have to get through this trip that I'm on, and then I'll be back."

"Forever?"

"Yup." He gulped down hard. "Forever."

"Daddy?"

"Yes, angel?"

"If you're not staying, why are you in your bathrobe then? Why aren't you wearing your work clothes?"

"Well, that was one of the reasons I came back—to get some clean clothes—but I didn't want to go to the bedroom and wake up Mommy."

"Or Mister O'Reilly, right?"

Cavanaugh looked at his daughter. He was surprised she knew. Then again, how could she not know?

"Yeah." He bit down on his lip. "Or Mister O'Reilly."

"Well, Mister O'Reilly keeps some of his clothes downstairs. Maybe you can borrow them."

"Wait—what? He keeps his clothes in our house? Downstairs?"

"Uh-huh. In the laundry room. Mommy and I—we washed and dried them together. Or, I mean, she really was the one who washed and dried them—I just helped her fold them, really. She says I'm a good folder."

"Bet you are, angel," said Cavanaugh. "I'll be sure to check that out. Thanks for the tip." He kissed the top of her head. "Alright, gotta go now. You should go back to sleep. You have school tomorrow."

She lowered her head, then looked back up at Cavanaugh.

"Honey? You *are* going to go to school tomorrow, aren't you?"

She shrugged. "I don't know. I guess."

"You should. You should see your classmates, hang out with your friends. I'm sure they must miss you dearly."

"How'd you know?"

"How'd I know what?"

"How'd you know that I haven't been at school?"

Cavanaugh just then realized that the only reason he knew was because the O'Reilly girl had told him. If he were to mention his visit to the O'Reilly house, then he knew that he might have to tell her about how he gave her previous bobblehead away.

"I just know, sweetheart," said Cavanaugh. "I'm your father."

She smiled coyly. "Oh. Okay."

"Come on," said Cavanaugh. "Let's get you back into bed."

"But, Daddy?"

"What is it, angel?"

"When do you think you'll be back?"

"Like I told you: soon."

"How soon?"

"Not sure how soon yet. But I'll let your mother know when I'm sure."

"Okay."

"Good night, angel."

"Good night, Daddy."

"I love you, angel."

"I love you, too, Daddy."

Cavanaugh kissed his daughter's forehead, and then turned and grabbed his briefcase. As he lifted the briefcase off the floor, his eye caught a glimpse of the bobblehead doll.

Still smirking.

Still mocking.

Still watching over.

He turned from the doll and headed toward the doorway.

"Daddy?"

Cavanaugh turned back and saw his daughter sitting up in her bed.

"Yes, angel?"

"Your head."

"My head?"

"Your head."

"What about my head?"

"Your head. It's no longer shaking like it was when I saw you in the window."

Cavanaugh placed his hand to his head. She was right: his head was now still. And it was all because of seeing her, he knew.

He smiled. "Alright, angel. Time for bed."

"Okay, Daddy."

"Sweet dreams, angel. Love you."

"Love you too, Daddy."

Cavanaugh turned again toward the doorway. He was just about to shut the door behind him, when his daughter called out to him yet again.

"Daddy?"

"Yes, angel?"

"What's a slider?"

"A what?"

"A slider. What is it?"

"Why do you want to—" But Cavanaugh already knew why she wanted to know. He set his briefcase back down on the floor and walked over to the bed.

"It's a type of breaking pitch," he said.

"What's a breaking pitch?"

"Here. I'll show you. Take off your socks. We'll roll them up and pretend it's a baseball."

"Okay, Daddy." The young girl smiled. Cavanaugh could see that she had lost another tooth while he was away.

She took off her socks and handed them to Cavanaugh, who rolled them up into the shape of a ball.

"Alright. Let's see here." He raised and gently bent her soft, little arm back behind her small, delicate ear, then cupped his hand over her hand, their separate shadows united as one against the wall.

Cavanaugh Cleans Up

Upon entering the laundry room downstairs, Cavanaugh found piles of men's clothing—T-shirts, sweatshirts, sweatpants, cargo pants, jeans, chinos, boxers, athletic socks, dress socks—that were not his own. Everything was neatly folded.

Mrs. Cavanaugh was right, thought Cavanaugh. Their little angel was a good folder, indeed.

There was not a single trace of anything that belonged to Cavanaugh in the room—not even a spare, old sock. The room was up to the brim with all things O'Reilly—as if he had been living in the Cavanaugh house forever. Cavanaugh remembered what Mrs. O'Reilly had said earlier—that O'Reilly did this sometimes, leaving without word for a few days—but seeing all the articles of clothing in the room, and how they were so carefully arranged, made Cavanaugh wonder if this was not some brief respite from the realities of life at home for O'Reilly, but rather a more permanent commitment.

Cavanaugh took off his bathrobe and undershirt and slowly removed his shamrock boxers, careful not to let any remaining debris scatter over the floor. The insides of his boxers were stained in yellow, orange and brown, but it appeared more or less dry to Cavanaugh, and, to his relief, free of any of the chunkier forms of fecal residue.

He grabbed a pair of boxers—the top pair from the pile—and put them on. They were light blue with silver ship anchors all over them. They were a little oversized on Cavanaugh, but having just rid himself of his own soiled pair, he found them to be a welcome change.

Next, he slipped into a washed-out sweatshirt with what appeared to be the name of an institute on it, one which he had never heard of—perhaps a vocational school, he figured.

Then came the pants. First, Cavanaugh tried on the sweatpants, but they were too long and loose on him. He then tried on a pair of jeans, followed by a pair of chinos, but they were both too tight around the calves.

Cavanaugh snatched a pair of gray cargo pants from the counter and held them up to his waist. He had not worn cargo pants in decades but figured they might be his last hope. He pushed his legs through the holes and pulled up the pants: they were not exactly a perfect fit—just ever so tight around the hips—but they were comfortable enough, and he knew they would do the job.

Finishing things off, Cavanaugh grabbed a pair of white athletic socks from the sock pile, hopping on one foot, then the other, as he pulled them over his feet.

With a complete set of fresh clothing on for the first time in weeks, Cavanaugh felt like a new man.

"Like O'Reilly," muttered the voice, but Cavanaugh cast that notion aside, as he picked up his shit-stained boxers from the floor by his fingertips and carried them out of the laundry room before heading toward the kitchen.

In the kitchen, Cavanaugh could see and smell all the traces of his order from TOMMY's: a pile of wing bones in a bowl, little containers of toppings and condiments gone empty, the crumbed remains of garlic fries, and, of course, six empty glass bottles of Sam Adams. He recalled how O'Reilly and Mrs. Cavanaugh had come directly into the den from the garage with Cavanaugh's daughter earlier, so they must have spared themselves the sight and stench of what he had left behind. Out of fear of the three of them coming down the stairs and seeing this spectacle, Cavanaugh decided it would be best—especially for his daughter, he figured—to remove it all entirely from the premises.

He opened one of the kitchen cabinet doors and pulled out an extra-large trash bag.

The first thing he tossed into the trash bag were the pair of shit-stained shamrock boxers. He then walked over to the round kitchen table and picked up all the empty containers, large and small, and tossed those into the trash bag as well. Next, he grabbed each empty bottle of Sam Adams, one by one, and placed them carefully into the trash bag so as not to stir anyone awake upstairs. Finally, he tipped the giant bowl of wing bones into the trash bag, and placed the bowl itself in the sink. He thought for a moment of placing the bowl in the dishwasher in order to better conceal any evidence of his presence, but between the articles of clothing he had already left behind in various rooms throughout the house and the debris that was surely scattered about the floor upstairs, he figured that the cat was already out of the bag.

Cavanaugh tied the top of the trash bag into a knot and was about to head out of the kitchen when he suddenly came to a halt. There, lying on the kitchen counter, were his wallet and house keys, and next to it, plugged into the wall, the neon-rainbow charger and phone. He grabbed his wallet and keys and pulled his phone and charger out of the jack, and stuffed them all into the spacious pockets of O'Reilly's cargo pants. He then picked up the trash bag again and exited the kitchen.

Waiting for him in the foyer at the foot of the staircase was his briefcase full of satin. Cavanaugh lifted the briefcase from the floor and was about to exit the front door—briefcase in one hand, trash bag in the other—when he suddenly imagined the wet and chilly conditions he was about to encounter, and figured it would be best not to go back and forth from the house but instead make it out of the house in one shot.

Cavanaugh placed the briefcase and trash bag on the floor and walked to the closet closest to the front door, where all the coats were kept. As he opened the closet, he had half-expected to find all his coats discarded and replaced by O'Reilly's coats, but instead he found three of his own coats—one for each season, except for the one he had been wearing for the weeks he was away, for that one had been left on the floor of the master bathroom—hanging in the same spot they had always hung.

There was also a windbreaker that was at first unfamiliar to him, but then he quickly recognized it: it was the windbreaker that O'Reilly had worn to the ballgame.

"Play ball," said the voice.

Cavanaugh grabbed his winter overcoat from the hanger, and put it on. Though it was not even close to winter yet, it was a very roomy coat, which, for his forthcoming travels, would be of good use to him.

"The more pocket room, the merrier," said the voice.

And with no telling how long his next round of meanderings would be, perhaps a winter overcoat was the sensible choice, figured Cavanaugh.

On the floor of the closet, next to a small, beaten-up suitcase that was not his own, were his old, worn-out running shoes. He had not gone out for a run in years, yet here he was: on the run.

With the laces already tied, Cavanaugh simply shoved his feet into the shoes.

"As good as new," said the voice.

Cavanaugh lifted the briefcase and trash bag off the floor again, then tiptoed his way to the doorway. As he turned the doorknob, the door jingled ever so softly.

Or was it the empty bottles inside the trash bag that jingled?

He was not sure which.

With briefcase in one hand and trash bag in the other, he exited the house, the door barely making a sound behind him as he finessed it closed with his foot.

He was a free man.

"A free agent," said the voice.

"An unrestricted free agent," said Cavanaugh.

A pencil-pusher with no pencils to push.

A number-cruncher with no numbers to crunch.

It was he, Cavanaugh, who was just a number now, a middling middle-aged middleman carrying a briefcase full of satin on the wide-open road.

He was not up.

He was not down.

He was now just Cavanaugh, plain and simple, and nothing else.

A husband with no wife to provide for.

A father with no child to care for.

A homeowner with no longer a house to keep and call his own.

He took a quick glance back over his shoulder, partly to see if anyone from inside the house was watching or coming up behind him, but also to take in what would perhaps be the last look at his home before he left it for good.

Nevertheless, his feet kept moving forward and this short look back did little to disrupt his brisk pace, as he headed down the pavement of the driveway. It felt good to him to feel the fresh air again, but it was not enough: something was percolating in his stomach anew.

When he got to the foot of the driveway, he placed his briefcase on the pavement and lifted the lid of the garbage bin. The bin was empty, but the air inside it had a particular acidic rank to it—a reeking of sorts from something, perhaps, recently disposed of—that filled his nostrils and seemed to compound that feeling of queasiness he had felt only hours earlier.

Cavanaugh hoisted the trash bag up over the rim of the bin, and as he attempted to let it drop to the bottom, that is when he felt it: a surge. A surge shooting upward, from the center of his body. It came out like water from a hose, projecting outward to both the inside and outside of the bin and onto the pavement around it.

And then there was a second surge.

And a third.

And a fourth.

It kept coming.

A creamy, yeasty blend of things recently consumed, some digested, some less so, all coated in a chunky broth of brown, yellow and orange—the stench of which only added to his nausea, thus extending this bout of barfing even further.

And there was blood—copious amounts of it—shooting out as well. Cavanaugh thought that perhaps it had been pushed out from his lungs or from excess bile inside his stomach, but as the blood dripped and drooled from his mouth between surges, he realized it was originating from a source closer to the surface: his gums.

Cavanaugh had all but ignored his oral hygiene in the weeks he had been away and this, he knew, was the culminating price.

The vomiting raged on for some time—it became more and more red as it went on—before it finally began to unwind, leaving Cavanaugh in a fit of shaking. His body jerked forward a couple of times more, but these concluding convulsions, he discovered, were just the minor tremors of aftershock.

How was the meat lasagna, Cavanaugh?

Standing upright now, Cavanaugh could see the thick, gastric stew of his own making sitting at the bottom of the bin and dripping from the bin's exterior. The pavement around the bin was also covered in puddles of digestive foam, his beloved briefcase just inches from range. A few small chunks had gotten on the lapel of his coat, and a couple of bits had landed on the tip of his running shoe, but other than that, he seemed to have gotten off scot-free.

Or had he?

Cavanaugh gazed at the house across the street, and looked up at the dimly-lit window of the top floor.

There it was again: the shadow. It had no eyes, but Cavanaugh knew it was watching and had been watching the moment he stepped out of the house.

"Fuck you, shadow. Fuck you. Fuck you. Fuck you."

Cavanaugh lifted the trash bag from the pavement—it had not successfully reached its target on the previous attempt—and dropped it down on top of the foamy pile of stew at the bottom of the bin.

"Well, that conceals most of it," said the voice. "What about the rest of it?"

Cavanaugh shrugged. "They'll never know it was me—they'll think it came from a raccoon or something."

"What about your shoe? Your lapel?"

Cavanaugh reached into the large pockets of his overcoat and pulled out a small, dusty packet of tissues that was barely half-full. He had always kept a packet inside his coat pocket during the cold winter months.

He extracted a tissue from the packet and brushed it about the front of his coat and shoe, carefully flicking off the gooey remains. He then took out another tissue and used it to wipe off the edges of his mouth and chin. With all residual evidence of regurgitation having been removed from his person, Cavanaugh rolled the two tissues together into a wad, crammed the wad into the bin, and then covered the bin with the lid.

He then picked up his briefcase off the pavement and gazed up at the window across the street again.

The shadow was still there.

Cavanaugh raised his middle finger up in the air, aiming it at the shadow.

"So long, shadow."

Cavanaugh stepped off the driveway and onto the sidewalk, his briefcase full of satin firmly in his grip, leaving behind whatever remaining articles, and particles, of evidence he left inside and outside the house to chance. With his body having emptied itself of its more disagreeable contents, Cavanaugh now found himself walking with an extra spring in his step, as he carefully averted the puddles scattered about the sidewalk and along the curb that were generated from the overnight rain. His mouth was still festering a bit, yet he still felt refreshed regardless, as something about the early morning air gave him a renewed sense of purpose.

Somewhere in the sky, the sun was rising.

Somewhere in a tree, a robin was singing.

Somewhere up the road, a dog barked.

Cavanaugh Reunites with an Old Friend

By the time Cavanaugh reached the O'Reilly property, the sun was halfway above the horizon, but the streetlamps along the road still flickered with life. Standing in front of the O'Reilly driveway, he could see that all the lights inside the house were off, and that there was the kind of stillness about the house that suggested that neither of its two current occupants had yet arisen.

Cavanaugh studied the house's gray exterior, its rectangular windows, its shoddy roofing. He wondered if either of those two current occupants had the faintest clue regarding the whereabouts of the man who did all he could to woo and win over their hearts, but was now trying his charms out on another mother-and-daughter duo down the block.

Cavanaugh was unsure about how to proceed.

Should I tell them? wondered Cavanaugh. Should I ring the doorbell, wake them up, and just tell them? Or should I wait for more signs of life inside—maybe wait for a light to flicker on or a window shade to pull up?

He stood there frozen on the sidewalk, mulling over some alternative ideas: Perhaps he should just send a text. Or maybe he should just write them a note, put it in an envelope, and place it in their mailbox—he would not even have to sign it, he figured.

Standing there alone in front of their driveway, with a streetlamp shining over him in the closing predawn minutes of early morning, Cavanaugh suddenly felt too exposed and decided to scram before someone caught him gawking and called the police. He had already caused enough disruption in people's lives. It was time to move on.

Cavanaugh was about to turn and continue his walk up the road, when something in the open garbage bin at the foot of the O'Reilly driveway caught his eye: it was the Brett Kavanaugh bobblehead doll—the one he had given to Cavanaugh's daughter and had accompanied him on his previous travels.

It was looking straight up toward the sky, wet and forlorn, having been laid atop a full bag of trash, level with the rim of the bin.

Cavanaugh placed his briefcase on the pavement, then leaned over the bin, lifting the bobblehead up from the heap.

The doll was drenched to its very bolts. It looked under duress to Cavanaugh—disheveled, battered, bruised. Its jawline was a tad askew, transforming its mischievous grin into a pitiable grimace. Its torso felt cold in Cavanaugh's hands, and the cool, crisp air seemed to make its lifeless body shiver in the breeze.

Cavanaugh wiped his old companion down with the lining of his overcoat until it was all dry, then hugged it close to his chest to warm it. From there, he lifted his discarded friend up to his face, and then, without merely a thought, he kissed the doll on its forehead.

This display of affection toward the Kavanaugh doll surprised even Cavanaugh himself. He looked around to see if anyone was watching, but there were no onlookers.

He looked back at the fractured face of the bobblehead.

"What goes around, comes around," said the voice.

Cavanaugh turned and lifted his briefcase off the pavement.

With his bobbleheaded friend back in one hand, and his briefcase full of satin in the other, Cavanaugh resumed his walk up the road, as the looming bright lights of the streetlamps flickered off, lamp by lamp, house by house.

Mrs. Cavanaugh Follows the Trail

Something inside the stomach of Mrs. Cavanaugh did not agree with her when she awoke. Was it the infidelity? Or was it just finding herself in bed next to a sleeping, snoring O'Reilly?

She got out from under the comforter and swung her feet off the bed, her breasts jiggling against one another, pale and naked. She was about to put her first foot on the floor when she saw something tiny and brown lying on top of the hardwood.

Boot against wood.

Belt against buckle.

Wasn't that what she often heard Cavanaugh mutter in his sleep? Or was it *belt against buckle* first, then *boot against wood*?

Mrs. Cavanaugh sat still for a moment and tried to remember but could not. She then leaned forward from the bed, and hunched herself over the floor to get a better look.

Must be a pebble or something, she figured. Or perhaps a clump of dry mud or dirt. Had she tracked it into the room from outside?

When she got herself fully off the bed and began to walk toward the master bathroom, she noticed more of the same debris she had seen when she first arose, but these bits varied in shape and size, and some were not as much brown as they were a dark orange, and they seemed to circle, like a trail, around the foot of the bed, toward the side where O'Reilly was still sound asleep.

She tiptoed around the scattered debris, moving carefully past the foot of the bed, her eyes never shifting their focus from the floor, her bare feet cold against the hardwood, following the trail all the way to the other side of the bed, toward the doorway, where she found, and almost stepped on if not for some fancy foot-maneuvering, the largest chunk of debris yet: an orangey-brown, slug-shaped morsel, lightly moist and moderately C-shaped.

Mrs. Cavanaugh stopped dead in her tracks when she saw this object, as she studied its contour and properties from above, before veering her eyes toward the man sleeping nearest to this most vile and mysterious of deposits.

He couldn't have, she thought.

She looked back at the large object on the floor.

It couldn't be.

Or could it?

She knew immediately what the object probably was, but she held out on the hope that perhaps it was just her eyes playing tricks on her, as they often did in the early morning hours.

What she needed now was confirmation.

Slowly, she bent forward, her face inching toward the floor, with one hand pulling her hair back behind her head into a bun so as not to allow it to make incidental contact with the object in question. When she got close enough, she took a small whiff.

The confirmation was instantaneous, and so, too, was the wave of nausea. She stumbled forward toward the bed, the bottom of her bare heel grazing the edge of a separate and smaller brown object.

She shouted right into O'Reilly's sleeping face. "Get—"

But before she could even say the word *out*, a pinkish-red avalanche of digestive juices flew up from the inside of her mouth, out onto the part of the cream-colored comforter that semi-covered O'Reilly's broad and freckled chest.

When she finished unloading, Mrs. Cavanaugh retreated from the bed, the residue of her purge trickling its way down from her chin, onto her fleshy and supple breasts. Gripping her elbows and shivering in the shadows of her bedroom, she gazed down at O'Reilly's tranquil face, as the first beams of sunlight eked their way through the window.

"O'Reilly," she whispered.

The man whose head was lying on the pillow that was once her husband's was still sound asleep, the pace and rhythm of his snoring unbroken.

"O'Reilly," she whispered again.

Was that a smile beginning to take shape on his slumbering face? Or were her eyes just playing—

No, they were not just playing tricks on her, she decided. As sure as that was his excrement scattered about the bedroom floor, they were not just playing tricks.

Something began to slowly surge upward again from the inside of the center of her body. Was it once again the sight and stench of the excrement that was causing it, or was it instead her new reality laying itself bare?

She leaned her face in closer to O'Reilly's face, awaiting what was rising inside her to shoot itself out from her outstretched mouth.

Perhaps this will do the trick this time, she thought.

Cavanaugh Stops for a Drink

She lived several towns over, at the last stop on the route. Her house was situated in the middle of the block, halfway up a hill—or halfway down it, depending on which way you were walking.

Cavanaugh was walking his way up the hill, his festering mouth and aching back notwithstanding, when the voice spoke out again.

"I could use a drink," it said.

This was the first time the voice had spoken since he had left his neighborhood and boarded the bus to begin his new journey.

When he reached the front of her house and rang the doorbell, she answered it so quickly that it made Cavanaugh wonder if she had been waiting for him there behind the door all along, expecting his return.

How many years had it been since he had last seen her? Cavanaugh pondered this as he studied the old yet familiar woman standing at the doorway in front of him.

She stared at him warily, looking him up and down. The foyer in which she stood was dark and shadowy, just as it had always been. Everything behind her ticked and hummed.

She had a barrette in her hair, that same one from that time she was—

"Can I help you?"

She did not recognize him. Was it her aging that caused her not to recognize him, or was it his own aging that caused it?

He said the first thing that popped into his head.

"Missus Cavanaugh?" *Missus Cavanaugh? Did I just really call her that?*

"Yes," said the voice, "You really *did* just call her that."

"Speaking," said the old woman.

"May I come in?"

"Come in?"

"Well, don't you recognize me?"

"Recognize you?"

"Yeah, recognize me. I'm your—"

"What's that your holding?"

"A briefcase."

"No, the other thing."

"A doll."

"A doll?"

"A bobblehead doll."

"What for?"

"I don't know. To keep me company, I guess."

"Oh, really?" said the old woman. "Well, I guess that makes sense. We could all use some company sometimes, I suppose—myself included. Very well then—come on in. If you would be so kind as to wipe your feet on the mat there, I'd appreciate it. Trying to keep the filth and germs out, if you don't mind."

Cavanaugh wiped his feet on the mat and followed the old woman down the narrow hallway of his youth, as it wound its way toward the kitchen.

Inside the kitchen, the ticking was louder, and so was the humming. There was a small eating table by the window.

"Here," said the old woman, pulling a wooden chair out from the table. "Have a seat."

Cavanaugh put his briefcase down and sat in the chair, the bobblehead doll atop his lap.

The old woman shuffled over to the refrigerator and opened it. On the outside of its door, hanging by a magnet, was a single photo: a smiling young, freckle-faced boy with a flowing mane of brown hair, wearing a denim jacket and blue jeans, sitting on the lap of a woman who looked much like the old woman but decades younger.

The old woman turned to face him again, her cheeks and forehead wrinkled and spotted, her chin shaggy and dimpled at the tip. The hair on her head was all white now—not the light shade of brown Cavanaugh had remembered.

There was a modest hump protruding from the top of her back.

"Lemonade or cider?"

"Lemonade," said Cavanaugh.

The old woman grabbed the carton of lemonade from the refrigerator, placed it on the table, then slowly shuffled back across the small room, toward the counter. When she reached the counter, she opened the cabinet above it, and drew out two drinking glasses. She then pulled out the chair opposite Cavanaugh, and slowly crouched herself down on its seat. She poured the lemonade into Cavanaugh's glass, then her own.

Cavanaugh raised his glass and took a sip, and the old woman followed suit.

"Hits the spot, doesn't it?"

Cavanaugh nodded, even though he didn't mean it. Without thinking, he reached into the pockets of O'Reilly's cargo pants: if only he had a flask with him so he could sneak a drop into his glass.

"Say," said the old woman, as she eyed Cavanaugh across the table. "You sort of look like how my husband used to look."

"You mean Mister Cavanaugh?"

Mister Cavanaugh? This was getting too weird.

"Yeah. Him. Mister Cavanaugh—or just plain Cavanaugh, which is what I used to always call him."

She took another sip and gazed out the window, its bottom slightly ajar. Cavanaugh could feel the ebb and flow of a gentle draft as he continued to take small sips from his glass.

The old woman sighed. "Yeah, Cavanaugh, Cavanaugh." She turned her gaze back to look squarely at Cavanaugh. "Hey, want to know what Cavanaugh means?"

Cavanaugh swished the lemonade in his mouth, gulped it down, then placed his glass on the table. He wanted to belch, but he held it in.

"Cavanaugh means something?"

"Sure, it means something," said the old woman. "It means 'born handsome'—or at least that's what my husband said it meant. He said the name came from some Old Gaelic surname that meant more or less the same thing: born handsome."

Cavanaugh stroked the pockmarks on his face with his fingers, felt the indents. "Born handsome," he whispered.

"Uh-huh. That's what he said. Born handsome." The old woman winked at Cavanaugh.

Cavanaugh raised his glass, took another sip, swished the lemonade around in his mouth again, then swallowed. He took a deep breath, then spoke.

"Missus Cavanaugh," said Cavanaugh, "what exactly happened with your husband?"

"What do you mean what happened?"

Cavanaugh carefully placed his glass back on the table. "Well, what I mean is, like, what ended up happening with him—like, where did he go?"

The old woman looked at Cavanaugh with the kind of warmth and tenderness that only a mother of an only child could offer. The familiar twinkle in her eye—it had come back, as if someone had suddenly turned the light back on inside her head.

"Well," said the old woman, "what ended up happening with him was—"

Something rumbled outside, beyond the window. Cavanaugh could hear the china inside the cupboard clatter, as the table vibrated in front of him. He and the old woman watched their glasses wobble, as their lemonades breached the rims.

Outside the window, a dog barked and a robin fluttered its wings.

Somewhere down the road, an engine roared. The sound it made grew louder and louder as it revved and thundered up the block.

The old woman leaned her head toward the window and listened. Something fell off the wall behind her shoulder—some woven artifact of sorts—but the old woman listened on regardless.

Cavanaugh sat still and listened as well. A draft much harsher than the one he had felt earlier blew in through the window screen, casting a chill through the insides of his body.

The ticking and humming echoed louder and louder against his eardrums. He hugged his doll tight against his gut.

"There goes your bus," said the old woman. She pulled her head back from the window and turned to face Cavanaugh. The twinkle in her eye was still there. "Better go catch it."

Cavanaugh Goes Uphill, Then Downhill, Then Back Up the Hill Again

Cavanaugh was back on the bus. It had been nearly two weeks since he had returned home, only to leave it again. Over that time period, he had not bathed, brushed his teeth, shaved his face, combed his hair, or changed a single article of clothing.

None of the other regulars on the bus—neither the driver nor the passengers—seemed to recognize him from his previous meanderings about town, for the clothes he wore now were not intended for him to wear, and his beard had now grown both long enough and thick enough to cover every mole and pockmark on his face.

The only clues that this Cavanaugh on the bus was the same Cavanaugh from those earlier wanderings were the bobblehead doll standing upright on the seat by his side and the briefcase sitting sideways on top of his lap as he slouched and slept through stop after stop.

There was also, of course, the fact that his head was twitching. Not to mention he was piss-drunk again—that was a dead giveaway as well. Yet, as always, no one paid much attention to Cavanaugh.

Passengers got on the bus.

Passengers got off the bus.

One driver made one set of stops.

Another driver made another set of stops.

Through it all, the bus drove on, uphill, then downhill, then back up the hill again.

When he awoke from his slumber, Cavanaugh found himself sitting across from a passenger reading a newspaper. The newspaper was held out in such a way by the passenger that Cavanaugh could not see the passenger's face.

Cavanaugh pulled a flask out from his overcoat, and took a long, hard sip. He had discovered early in the course of this new round of meanderings that the deep pockets of his overcoat, as well as those found in O'Reilly's cargo pants, were amenable to holding several flasks at once. As far as Cavanaugh was concerned, bottles and cans were now a thing of the past.

The bus bumped and thumped along its hillocky and circuitous route, causing some of the contents inside Cavanaugh's flask to dribble out onto his beard and overcoat.

"Sure is a bumpy ride, ain't it?" said Cavanaugh to the passenger behind the newspaper.

But the passenger offered no reply, and the newspaper that the passenger held remained locked in its position.

Cavanaugh looked at his bobbleheaded companion sitting by his side. He had replaced its dead batteries with new ones he had purchased just days after he had returned to his travels.

Now was a good time to test them out, he figured.

Cavanaugh lifted the bobblehead from its seat and placed it on his lap, on top of the briefcase. He then pressed the button on its base, and watched its head begin to bobble.

He turned and looked across the aisle.

The passenger behind the newspaper bounced along with the rhythm of the bus, but otherwise offered no response.

Must be a different passenger behind the newspaper from the one that was behind the newspaper the last time around, figured Cavanaugh.

Cavanaugh gazed out the window. What was once alien to him had now become familiar.

The bars.

The bodegas.

The boutiques.

The motels.

The restaurants.

The plazas.

The strip malls.

The strip clubs.

Through the glass, Cavanaugh could see the sign he had been waiting for, just a few blocks up the road, its neon-blue lights flickering on, then off, then on again under the red evening sky.

"Wrong Way Corrigan's," muttered Cavanaugh, reading the sign.

Every time the WRONG WAY part of the sign flickered on, the CORRIGAN'S part of the sign flickered off, and every time the WRONG WAY part flickered off, the CORRIGAN'S part flickered on.

The bus stopped at the station across from Corrigan's and the doors swung open. The driver announced the cross street, but Cavanaugh remained seated. He had not paid a visit to Corrigan's since the last time the waitress told him to hit the road.

The driver pulled the lever again and the doors of the bus closed shut. The bus continued on, uphill, then downhill, then back up the hill again.

Cavanaugh gulped down the remaining contents inside his flask, stuffed the tin piece into his overcoat, then reached into the pockets of O'Reilly's cargo pants and pulled out a new one.

He unscrewed the cap and took a swig, and was about to follow it up with another swig, when, suddenly, the bus went over a large bump, almost tossing the flask out from under his grip.

The jolt of the bump jostled the bobblehead back to life on Cavanaugh's lap, and the head began to bobble once again.

A sound came from across the aisle—a jingling.

A jingling and a wheezing.

A wheezing and a snorting.

It was the passenger behind the newspaper. Cavanaugh watched him as he swung forward then back, back then forward, stomping his work boots over and over in a convulsive fit of laughter, the newspaper still firm in his grip, never budging from the front of his face.

On and on, the passenger stomped and jingled, jingled and stomped, as the head of the bobblehead bobbled and snapped, snapped and bobbled.

Belt against buckle.

Boot against wood.

Guess it's the same passenger after all, figured Cavanaugh.

When the bobbling of the bobblehead came to an end, so too did the wheezing, snorting, stomping and jingling from the passenger behind the newspaper. Cavanaugh was about to press the button down again, but then decided that such a routine had already become tiresome.

Cavanaugh closed the cap on his flask and shoved it back into O'Reilly's cargo pants. He leaned his ear against the window, closed his eyes, and listened as hard as he could to the sounds coming from the other side of the glass.

A bell ringing.

A bird singing.

A door creaking.

A wheel squeaking.

A horn beeping.

A child weeping.

A lone dog barking down the road.

Acknowledgments

THE AUTHOR OF THIS BOOK wishes to thank Jacob Smullyan and Sagging Meniscus Press for publishing his fiction again, and for giving the voices inside his head the opportunity to be heard. He would also like to thank the three angels of his life—his wife, Jennifer, and his two sons, Zachary and Samuel—for their love and affection, and for always making home feel like home.

JOSHUA KORNREICH is the author of *The Boy Who Killed Caterpillars* (Marick, 2007; Dzanc, 2013); *Knotty, Knotty, Knotty* (Black Mountain, 2014); *Horsebuggy* (Sagging Meniscus, 2019); *Cavanaugh* (Sagging Meniscus, 2021); and *Shakes Bear in the Dark* (Sagging Meniscus, 2022). He lives in New York City with his wife and two sons.

BLANK PAGE BOOKS

are dedicated to the memory of Royce M. Becker,
who designed Sagging Meniscus books from 2015–2020.

They are:

IVÁN ARGÜELLES
THE BLANK PAGE

JESI BENDER
KINDERKRANKENHAUS

MARVIN COHEN
BOOBOO ROI
THE HARD LIFE OF A STONE, AND OTHER THOUGHTS

GRAHAM GUEST
HENRY'S CHAPEL

JOSHUA KORNREICH
CAVANAUGH
SHAKES BEAR IN THE DARK

STEPHEN MOLES
YOUR DARK MEANING, MOUSE

M.J. NICHOLLS
CONDEMNED TO CYMRU

PAOLO PERGOLA
RESET

BARDSLEY ROSENBRIDGE
SORRY, I BROKE YOUR PROMISE

CHRISTOPHER CARTER SANDERSON
THE SUPPORT VERSES

CPSIA information can be obtained
at www.ICGtesting.com
Printed in the USA
LVHW092016240921
698682LV00002B/169